FOREWORD

irst published between 1971 and 1981, Michael Moorcock's *The Warlord of the Air* (or is it *The War Lord of the Air?*— editions vary), *The Land Leviathan* and *The Steel Tsar*—three books known collectively as "The Oswald Bastable Trilogy" or "A Nomad of the Time Streams"—look backwards, forwards and sideways at the same time.

In 1969, there were people going around seriously saying that science fiction would die as a genre after the moon landing. The future was here, so we didn't need to think about it any more. Certainly, the genre had been around long enough by then for its earlier examples to seem comically outdated—all those books and stories where there's a breathable atmosphere on the moon, or astro-navigators fiddle with slide rules on their faster-than-light spaceships. Still, there were people who saw the beauty and the terror and (most importantly) the continued relevance of the futures which didn't happen.

In Moorcock's novels, army officer Oswald Bastable—the name comes from a series of books by E. Nesbit, author of *Five Children and It*—comes unstuck in time from his own era (1903) and tours three overlapping, yet different, imagined versions of the twentieth century… where the British Empire persists into the 1970s, technological advances lead to a war that leaves the world in ruins in the early 1900s and a Russian revolution did not lead to a Soviet state. Constant in all these fractured mirrors of our own history are airships, stately hold-overs from the exciting books of Jules Verne (*The Clipper of the Clouds*) and George Griffith (*The Angel of the Revolution*), and the atomic bomb (which arrived in fiction in 1914 in H.G. Wells' *The World Set Free*). The point is not, as in some meticulously constructed and argued alternative histories, to imagine how things might have been, but to confront the way things really were, as our collective urges for incompatible utopias brought about horrors beyond imagining. Though not averse to blaming individuals, these books are strong on collective responsibility: there are versions here of Joseph Stalin, Ronald Reagan, Enoch Powell and Harold Wilson, as sad little men whose small-minded blind spots, ambitions and cruelties bring about personal and global disasters. But no one is let off the hook, and we're all to blame.

The voice of these novels is a perfect match for the Victorian and Edwardian authors evoked over and over in them… not just Wells, Nesbit and Griffith, but Rider Haggard, Conan Doyle, Rudyard Kipling (*With the Night Mail*), Saki (*When William Came*—a novel Moorcock brought back into print in the anthology *England Invaded*), George Tomkyns Chesney (*The Battle of Dorking*) and many other scientific romancers of the nineteenth and early twentieth centuries. Moorcock can embrace, with love, the idealism and imagination expressed in these writers' works, though as many were catastrophists as utopians, but recognizes that they share in the collective responsibility for the way the world really turned out. A key influence on the steampunk movement in contemporary fantasy, these books are spikier, more clear-sighted and complicated than most superficially similar visions of technological Victoriana.

A NOMAD OF THE TIME STREAMS NOVEL

THE THIRD ADVENTURE

THE STEEL TSAR

ALSO AVAILABLE FROM TITAN BOOKS

A NOMAD OF THE TIME STREAMS

The Warlord of the Air
The Land Leviathan

A NOMAD OF THE TIME STREAMS NOVEL

THE THIRD ADVENTURE

THE STEEL TSAR

THIRD VOLUME IN THE
OSWALD BASTABLE TRILOGY

MICHAEL MOORCOCK

TITAN BOOKS

The Steel Tsar
Print edition ISBN: 9781781161470
E-book edition ISBN: 9781781161500

Published by Titan Books
A division of Titan Publishing Group Ltd
144 Southwark Street, London SE1 0UP

First edition: August 2013
1 3 5 7 9 10 8 6 4 2

Michael Moorcock asserts the moral right to be identified as the author of this work.
Copyright © 1981, 2013 by Michael Moorcock.
Foreword copyright © 2013 by Kim Newman.

Edited by John Davey.

A CIP catalogue record for this title is available from the British Library.

Printed and bound in the United States.

*For all who died at Babi Yar and for
Anatoly Kuznetsov, who died speaking the truth
and whose work was stolen by a liar*

These books are Griffith-like yarns—full of scrapes, adventures, exotica, jokes, plot reversals and charm—but they're at heart serious, sobering visions. I am delighted they are available again, and so will you be.

KIM NEWMAN

London, 2012

BOOK ONE

AN ENGLISH AIRSHIPMAN'S ADVENTURES IN THE GREAT WAR OF 1941

CHAPTER ONE

The Manner of My Dying

It was, I think, my fifth day at sea when the revelation came. Just as at some stage of his existence a man can reach a particular decision about how to lead his life, so can he come to a similar decision about how to encounter death. He can face the grim simple truth of his dying, or he can prefer to lose himself in some pleasant fantasy, some dream of heaven or of salvation, and so face his end almost with pleasure.

On my sixth day at sea it was obvious that I was to die and it was then that I chose to accept the illusion rather than the reality.

I had lain all morning at the bottom of the dugout. My face was pressed against wet, steaming wood. The tropical sun throbbed down on the back of my unprotected head and blistered my withered flesh. The slow drumming of my heart filled my ears and counterpointed the occasional slap of a wave against the side of the boat.

All I could think was that I had been spared one kind of death in order to die alone out here on the ocean. And I was grateful for that. It was much better than the death I had left behind.

Then I heard the cry of the seabird and I smiled a little to myself. I knew that the illusion was beginning. There was no possibility that I was in sight of land and therefore I could not really have heard a bird. I had had many similar auditory hallucinations in recent days.

I began to sink into what I knew must be my final coma. But the cry grew more insistent. I rolled over and blinked in the white glare of the sun. I felt the boat rock crazily with the movement of my thin body. Painfully I raised my head and peered through a shifting haze of silver and blue and saw my latest vision. It was a very fine one: more prosaic than some, but more detailed, too.

I had conjured up an island. An island rising at least a thousand feet out of the water, about ten miles long and four miles wide: a monstrous pile of volcanic basalt, limestone and coral, with deep green patches of foliage on its flanks.

I sank back into the dugout, squeezing my eyes shut and congratulating myself on the power of my own imagination. The hallucinations improved as any hopes of surviving vanished. I knew it was time to give myself up to madness, to pretend that the island was real and so die a pathetic rather than a dignified death.

I chuckled. The sound was a dry, death rattle.

Again the seabird screamed.

Why rot slowly and painfully for perhaps another thirty hours when I could die now in a comforting dream of having been saved at the last moment?

With the remains of my strength I crawled to the stern and grasped the starting cord of the outboard. Weakly I jerked at it. Nothing happened. Doggedly, I tried again. And again. And all the while I kept my eyes on the island, waiting to see if it would shimmer and disappear before I could make use of it.

I had seen so many visions in the past few days. I had seen milk-white angels with crystal cups of pure water drifting just out of my reach. I had seen blood-red devils with fiery pitch-forks piercing my skin. I had seen enemy airships which popped like bubbles just as they were about to release their bombs on me. I had seen orange-sailed schooners as tall as the Empire State Building. I had seen schools of tiny black whales. I had seen rose-coloured coral atolls on which lounged beautiful young women whose faces turned into the faces of Japanese soldiers as I came closer and who then slid beneath the waves where I was sure they were trying to capsize my boat. But this mirage retained its clarity no matter how hard I stared and it was so much more detailed than the others.

The engine fired after the tenth attempt to start it. There was hardly any fuel left. The screw squealed, rasped and began to turn. The water foamed. The boat moved reluctantly across a flat sea of burnished steel, beneath a swollen and throbbing disc of fire which was the sun, my enemy.

I straightened up, squatting like a desiccated old toad on the floor of the boat, whimpering as I gripped the tiller, for its touch sent shards of fire through my hand and into my body.

Still the hallucination did not waver; it even appeared to grow larger as I approached it. I completely forgot my pain as I allowed myself to be deceived by this splendid mirage.

I steered under brooding grey cliffs which fell sheer into the sea. I came to the lower slopes of the island and saw palms, their trunks bowed as if in prayer, swaying over sharp rocks washed by white surf. There was even a brown crab scuttling across a rock; there was weed and lichen of several varieties; seabirds diving in the shallows and darting upwards with shining fish in their long beaks. Perhaps the island was real, after all…?

But then I had rounded a coral outcrop and at once discovered the final confirmation of my complete madness. For here was a high concrete wall: a harbour wall encrusted above the water line with barnacles and coral and tiny plants. It had been built to follow the natural curve of a small bay. And over the top of the wall I saw the roofs and upper storeys of houses which might have belonged to a town on any part of the English coast. And as a superb last touch there was a flagpole at which flew a torn and weather-stained Union Jack! My fantasy was complete. I had created an English fishing port in the middle of the Indian Ocean.

I smiled again. The movement caused the blistered skin of my lips to crack still more. I ignored the discomfort. Now all I had to do was enter the harbour, step off onto what I believed to be dry land—and drown. It was a fine way to die. I gave another hoarse, mad chuckle, full of self-admiration, and I abandoned myself to the world of my mind.

Guiding my boat round the wall I found the harbour mouth. It was partly blocked by the wreck of a steamer. Rust-red funnels and masts rose above the surface. The water was unclouded and as I passed I could see the rest of the sunken ship leaning on the pink coral with multicoloured fish swimming in and out of its hatches and portholes. The name was still visible on her side: *Jeddah*, Manila.

Now I saw the little town quite clearly.

The buildings were in that rather spare Victorian or Edwardian neo-classical style and had a distinctly run-down look about them. They seemed deserted and some were obviously boarded up. Could I not perhaps create a few inhabitants before I died? Even a lascar or two would be better than nothing, for I now realized that I had built a typical Outpost of Empire. These were colonial buildings, not English ones, and there were square, largely undecorated native buildings mixed in with them.

On the quay stood various sheds and offices. The largest of these bore the faded slogan *Welland Rock Phosphate Mining*

Company. A nice touch of mine. Behind the town stood something resembling a small and pitted version of the Eiffel Tower. A battered airship mooring mast! Even better!

Out from the middle of the quay stretched a stone mole. It had been built for engine-driven cargo ships, but there were only a few rather seedy-looking native fishing dhows moored there now. They looked hardly seaworthy. I headed towards the mole, croaking out the words of the song I had not sung for the past two days.

"Rule Britannia, Britannia rules the waves! Britons never, never shall be—marr-I-ed to a mer-MI-ad at the bottom of the deep, blue sea!"

As if invoked by my chant Malays and Chinese materialized on the quayside. Some of them began to run along the jetty, their brown and yellow bodies gleaming in the sunshine, their thin arms gesticulating. They wore loincloths or sarongs of various colours and their faces were shaded by wide coolie hats of woven palm-leaves. I even heard their voices babbling in excitement as they approached.

I laughed as the boat bumped against the weed-grown jetty. I tried to stand up to address these wonderful creatures of my imagination. I felt godlike, I suppose. And to talk to them was the least, after all, that I could do.

I opened my mouth. I spread my arms.

"My friends—"

And my starved body collapsed under me. I fell backwards into the dugout, striking my shoulder on the empty petrol can which had contained my water.

There came a few words shouted in pidgin English and a brown figure in patched white shorts jumped into the canoe which rocked violently, jolting the last tatters of sense from my skull.

White teeth grinned. "You okay now, sar."

"I can't be," I said.

"Jolly good, sar."

Red darkness came.

I had set off to sail over a thousand miles to Australia in an open boat. I had barely managed to make two hundred, and most of that in the wrong direction.

The date was 3rd May, 1941. I had been at sea for about a hundred and fifty hours. It was three months since the Destruction of Singapore by the Third Fleet of the Imperial Japanese Aerial Navy.

CHAPTER TWO

The Destruction of Singapore

It had been a Utopia of sorts which the Japanese destroyed.

Designed as a model for other great settlements which would in the future spring up throughout the East, Singapore's white graceful skyscrapers, her systems of shining monorails, her complex of smoothly run airparks, had been lovingly laid out as an example to our Empire's duskier citizens of the benefits which British rule would eventually bring them.

And Singapore was burning. I am probably the last European to have witnessed her destruction.

After serving on the Portuguese aerial freighter *Palmerin* for a couple of months, I took several berths for single voyages, usually filling in for sick men, or men on leave, until I found myself in Rangoon without any chance of a job. I ran out of money in Rangoon and was willing to begin any kind of employment, even considered enlisting as a private in the army, when I was told by one of my bar acquaintances of a mate's position which had become vacant the night before.

"Chap was killed in a fight in Shari's house," he said,

nodding down the street. "The skipper started the fight. He's not offering good money, but it could get you somewhere better than Rangoon, eh?"

"Indeed."

"He's just over there? Want to meet him?"

I agreed. And that was how I came, eventually, to Singapore, though not in the ship on which I had signed.

A greasy Greek merchantman, the *Andreas Papadakis*, from some disgusting Cypriot port, trading in any marginally lucrative cargo which more fastidious captains would reject, had originally been bound for Bangkok when her engines had given out during an electrical storm which also affected our wireless telephone. We had drifted for two days, trying to make repairs aloft and losing two of our crew in the process, by the time the old windbag began to sag badly in the middle and drift towards the ground.

The *Papadakis* was not much suited to rough weather of any kind and could not be relied upon in even a minor crisis. The gondola cables and our steering cables both were badly in need of repair and we should have waited our moment and come down over water if we hoped for any chance of landing without serious damage, but by now the captain was drunk on retsina and refused to listen to my advice, while the rest of the crew, a mixed bunch of cut-throats from most parts of the Adriatic, were in a panic. I did my best to persuade the captain to let go our remaining gas, but he told me he knew best. The result was that we had begun to drop rapidly as we neared the coast of the Malay Peninsula, the *Andreas Papadakis* groaning and complaining the whole time and threatening to come apart at the seams.

She shivered and trembled in every section as the captain stared blearily through the forward ports and began, it seemed to me, to argue in Greek with the powers of Fate, on whom he blamed the entire disaster. It was as if he thought he could talk or soothe his way out of the inevitable fact. I kept my hands on the wheel, praying to sight a lake or at least a river, but we were heading over dense jungle. I remember a mass of waving green branches, an appalling screech of metal and wood as they met, a blow to my ribs which knocked me backwards into the arms of the captain, who must have died muttering some wretched Cypriot remonstration.

He saved my life, as it happened, by cushioning my own fall and breaking his back. I came to once or twice while I was being pulled from the wreckage, but only really regained my senses when I woke up in St. Mary's Hospital, Changi, Singapore. I had a few broken bones, which were mending, some minor internal injuries, which had been tended to, and I would soon be recovered, thanks to the Airshipmen's Distress Fund which had paid for my medical treatment and the period during which I would recuperate.

I had been lucky. There were only two other survivors. Five more had died in one of the native hospitals to which they had been taken.

While I rested, somewhat relieved not to be worrying about work and glad to be in Singapore, where there was every chance of finding decent employment, I began to read about the tensions growing between several of the Great Powers. Japan was disputing territory with Russia. The Russians, even though they were now a republic, had quite as much imperial determination as the Japs. However, we knew nothing of the War until the night of 22nd February, 1941: the night of the attack by Japan's Third Fleet: the night when a British dream of Utopia was destroyed perhaps for ever.

We were trying to escape what was left of the colony. An ambulance ship was moored to an improvised mast and the vessel all but filled the blackened, ruined grounds of St.

Mary's: a huge airship silhouetted against a sky which was ruby red with the flames of a thousand fires. The scene was surreal. I think of it today as the flight from Sodom and Gomorrah, but in Noah's Ark! Tiny figures of patients and staff rushed, panic-stricken, into the vessel's swollen belly while everywhere overhead moved monstrous, implacable Japanese flying ironclads. They had come suddenly, mindless beasts of the upper regions, to seed Singapore with their incendiary spawn.

Our resistance had been impotent. Far away a few searchlight beams wandered about the sky, sometimes showing a dense cloud of smoke from which could be glimpsed a section of one of the vast aerial men-o'-war. Then the three remaining anti-aircraft guns would boom and send up shells which either missed or exploded harmlessly against the side of the attacking craft. There were several of our monoplanes still buzzing through the blackness at speeds of over four hundred miles an hour, firing uselessly into hulls stronger than steel. They were picked off by tracer bullets shrieking from armoured gun-gondolas. I saw a hovergyro whirl like a frightened humming bird out of the flames, then it, too, was struck by magnesium bullets and went spinning into the flaming chaos below.

Our ship was not the latest type. Few hospital ships ever were. The cigar-shaped hull protecting the gasbags was of strong boron-fibreglass, but the two-tiered gondola below was more vulnerable. This gondola contained crew and passenger accommodation, engines, fuel and ballast tanks, and into it we were packing as many human beings as we could. I, of course, almost fully recovered, was helping the doctors and medical staff.

Without much hope of the ship's being able to get away, I helped carry stretchers up one of the two folding staircases lowered from the bowels of the ship. This in itself was a hard enough task, for the vessel was insecurely anchored and it swayed and strained at the dozen or so steel cables holding it to the ground.

The last terrified patient was packed in and the last nurses, carrying bundles of blankets and medical supplies, hurried aboard while airmen unpegged the gangways so they could be folded back into the ship. The stairs began to bounce like a cakewalk at a fair as, with the riggers, I managed to climb into the ship, losing my footing several times, shaken so much I felt my body would fall to pieces.

Suddenly several incendiary bombs struck the hospital at once. The darkness exploded with shouting flame. More bombs burst in the grounds, but incredibly none hit the airship direct. For a moment I was blinded by brilliant silver light and a wave of intense heat struck my face and hands.

From somewhere above I heard the captain shout "Let slip!" even before the gangway was fully raised. I clutched and found a handrail, dropped the box I had been carrying and desperately tried to grope my way up the few final rungs before I should be crushed by the automatically closing steps. My vision returned quickly and I saw the cables lashing as if in fury at having to release their grip on the ship. And then I stood on the embarkation platform itself and my immediate danger was past.

CHAPTER THREE

The Crash

Not much later I sighted the large conglomeration of tightly crowded together buildings which was the port of Surabaya. A busy city of mixed European and Malayan architecture, it was one of the few big ports to survive the decline of conventional shipping in favour of the air-going cargo vessels. Its harbour was still crammed with steamers and the whole place looked unnaturally peaceful in the early morning light. I felt an irrational surge of jealousy, a desire that Surabaya too might one day experience what Singapore had experienced. What right had this dirty, ugly port to survive when a mighty monument to a humane and idealistic Empire had perished in flames?

I pushed these dreadful ideas from my head. In a few more moments we should be crashing into the sea. Without power of any kind, the ship was going to have great difficulty in landing short of the harbour itself.

The whole vessel suddenly shuddered and I called for the staff to stand by as some patients began to moan questions or whimper in fear. The ship turned and began to drift in a clumsy, barely controlled manoeuvre and I lost sight of the town altogether. I saw only a steam launch surging over the waves and turning to follow us, leaving a white scar in the sea. There came a peculiar creaking and groaning from overhead as if some unusual strain had been placed on the gasbags and the hull containing them.

We began to drop.

A wailing went up from the patients then and we did our best to reassure them that everything was in order and that soon they would be in safe hospital beds in Surabaya.

I saw the sea shoot up to meet us and then retreat again. We began to move in a series of shuddering leaps as if riding a gigantic switchback. Somewhere a whole collection of crockery smashed to the deck and it was all I could do to hold myself upright by the safety rail.

And then, to my horror, I saw the roofs of the city below. Our gondola was almost scraping the highest of the buildings as we sped over them. We had missed the sea altogether and were traveling rapidly inland! The captain had left his decision until it was too late.

I heard the intercom buzz and then came the first officer's strained tones. A sudden strong following wind had blown up just as we were about to descend and this had completely thrown out everyone's calculations. The captain intended to try to take the ship right across the island and land in the sea near Djogjakarta, which was the nearest town we were likely to reach, considering the present direction of the wind. However, a lot of gas had already been valved out and we might not be able to gain enough height. In that event we must be prepared for a crash-landing on the ground.

I well knew what that would mean. The ship was considerably overburdened. If she fell from the sky to the land there was every chance we should all be killed.

A patient, wakened from sedation by the first officer's voice, screamed in alarm. A nurse hurried to soothe him.

The ship shivered and her nose came up sharply so that the deck tilted at a steep angle. Then the nose dipped and a few objects not secured began to slide down towards the bow. I jammed my foot against the rail. Through the ports I saw a Dutch flying boat follow us as if trying to make out the reason for our change of plan. Then, perhaps despairing of us, it turned back towards the sea.

Surabaya was behind us. Below us now lay a wide expanse of neat rice paddies, rows of tamarind trees and fields of tall sugar cane. We were so low that I could make out the heads of peasants looking up at us as our shadow moved across their fields. Then I was thrown against the rail as a fresh gust of wind caught the ship and slewed round again, revealing the kapok plantations on the slopes of Java's grim volcanic hillsides.

I thought we were bound to crash into the hills, for they were rising steeply and were beginning to turn into the grey flanks of mountains. From some of these drifted wisps of yellowish white smoke. Instinctively I braced myself, but we just managed to cross the first line of mountains. And ahead I could see denser clouds of pale grey smoke, coiling and boiling like a tangle of lazy serpents.

The ship jerked her nose up again and we ascended a few feet. The damaged tailplanes caused us to make a crazy zigzag over the landscape and I could see our elongated shadow moving erratically below. Then our motion steadied, but it seemed inevitable to me that we must soon crash into one of the many semi-active volcanoes which dominated Java's interior.

I was unprepared for the next lurch and I lost my grip on the rail as we started to go up rapidly. Clambering to my feet I saw that the ship had released her water ballast. It sprayed like a sudden rainstorm over the dusty slopes of the mountains. Perhaps, after all, we would make the sea on the other side.

But a few moments later the captain's voice came through the loudspeakers. It was calm enough under the circumstances. It told us that we were going to have to lighten the ship as much as possible. We were to make ready all non-essential materials and the crew would collect them from us in a couple of minutes.

Frantically we stumbled about the ward gathering up everything which could be thrown overboard. Eventually we had handed to the airshipmen a great pile of books, food, medical supplies, clothing, bedding, oxygen cylinders and more. All went overboard.

And the ship rose barely enough to clear the next range of mountains.

I wondered if the captain would ask for volunteers to jump from the ship next. We were by this time flying over a bleak and barren wasteland of cold lava ridges, with not so much as a clump of palms to break our descent should we crash. The tension in the wards had increased again and those patients not still asleep were talking in high, panicky voices.

Some of the questions were difficult to answer. Among the "non-essential" materials taken from us had been the bodies of those who had died in transit.

But even this act of desperate callousness had bought us very little time.

The intercom crackled again. The first officer began to speak. "Please ready yourselves for—Oh, God!"

The next moment I saw the grey mountainside rushing towards us and before we fully realized it, we were engulfed in clouds of grey-white smoke and our keel was making a frightful screaming sound as it scraped the sides of the cliff.

The screams of the patients joined the scream of the ship itself. I heard a monstrous creaking noise and then I was flung away from the rail and felt myself sliding towards the bunks.

The vessel bounced and juddered, seemed to gain height for

a moment and then came down with a horrifying crack which sent the bunks crashing loose from their moorings. I had the impression of waving arms and legs, of terrified faces. I heard trays of instruments clattering and saw bodies flying about like rag dolls. A great wail filled my ears and then the ship rolled, went up again and came down for the last time. In a flailing mass of bodies I was flung towards the starboard side. I saw my head rushing towards a fibreglass strut near the observation ports. I tried to put out my hands to stop the impact, but they were trapped by the bodies and objects on top of me. There came the final crash of impact and I remember being filled with an almost cheerful sense of relief that I had been killed and the ordeal was over at last.

CHAPTER FOUR

Prisoners

I think I must have awakened briefly once and heard peculiar squeaky voices babbling from somewhere far away and I realized that the gas was escaping and thus causing the speakers to talk in high-pitched tones. Deciding that I was alive and sure to be rescued, I fell back into unconsciousness.

When I next awoke I tried to move but could not. I thought that perhaps my back was broken, for there was little sensation save for the impression that something heavy was pressing down on me. Because of this pressure I found it very difficult to breathe in deeply enough to shout for the help that I was sure must be near, for I could hear people moving about quite close by.

The voices were no longer squeaky but they were not familiar either. I listened carefully. The voices were shouting some variant of Malay difficult for me to understand. I thought at first that the local peasantry, the sulphur-gatherers who work the volcanoes, had come to rescue us. I could smell the acrid smoke and it made breathing even harder. My next attempt to cry out failed. Then I heard more shouts.

And the shouts were followed by sharp reports which I did recognize. Gun shots.

With a feeling of terrible impotence I tried to move my head to see what was happening.

The shouting stopped. There was a stillness. Then a thin, hysterical scream. Another shot. Silence. A Malay voice giving rapid, savage commands.

Painfully, at last, I managed to turn my head and peer out of a jumble of twisted struts and wreckage. I saw bodies impaled on jagged shards of fibreglass and beyond them a pall of smoke through which dim figures moved. As the smoke cleared I saw bright flashes of green, red and yellow silk. These Malays were not sulphur-gatherers, that was certain.

Then I saw them clearly. They were clad in the familiar style of Malay bandits and pirates from Koto Raja to Timor. They wore richly coloured sarongs and embroidered jackets. On their heads were pitjis, turbans or wide coolie hats. There were sandals of painted leather on their brown feet and their bodies were crossed with bandoliers of cartridges. At their belts hung holstered revolvers, knives and parangs and they had rifles in their hands. I saw one come towards me, a look of cruel hatred frozen on his features. I dropped my head and shut my eyes, hearing him poke about in the wreckage above me. I heard a shot close to my face and thought he had fired at me, but the bullet landed in a corpse lying on top of me. He moved away.

I looked up again.

The bandits were herding the survivors down the mountain. Through the smoke I could see nurses in smudged, torn white uniforms, doctors still dressed in medical overalls or in shirtsleeves, airshipmen in sky blue, staggering ahead of their captors. But there were no patients among them. I watched in dazed despair until the smoke swallowed them up.

Then slowly, as it dawned on me what had happened to my

companions, pain began to flood through my body. I strained to twist myself round and see what pinned me in the wreckage.

One of the relatively light bunks had fallen on top of me and in the bunk was the body of a child. Its dead face, the eyes wide open, stared into mine. I shuddered and tried to lift the bunk clear. It moved slightly. The child's head rolled. I turned, reached out with bleeding hands and grasped a broken strut in front of me, pulling myself desperately from under the bunk until I was free and my breathing was easier. But my legs were still numb and I could not stand. I leaned forward and got a hold on another strut, using that to pull my body a few more inches over the wreckage, then I think I fainted for a few minutes.

It took me a long time to pull myself over the struts and the broken slabs of hull and the corpses until I lay on the outer areas of the wreckage on hard stone.

For all I was bruised and bleeding, I had no bones broken. The bodies of those who had died had saved me from the worst of the impact. Gradually the feeling came back to my legs and I was able to stand, gritting my teeth against the pain. I looked around me.

I was standing by the main wreckage of the ship on a mountain coated with streamers of yellow sulphur dust. Everywhere were bodies—crumpled, broken bodies of men, women and children, of patients in nightgowns and pyjamas, of wounded soldiers in tattered uniforms, of airship officers and crewmen, of nurses, orderlies and doctors. Nearly two thousand bodies and not one of them stirred as the wind moved the slow smoke over them, and the yellow dust swirled, and shreds of fabric fluttered amongst the crumpled ruins of the giant airship. Without hope I wandered through the piles of dead. Two thousand human beings who had sought to escape death in the fires of Singapore, only to find it on the barren, windswept rocks of an unknown Javanese hillside. I sighed and sat down, picking up a crushed packet of cigarettes I had seen. I opened the packet and took out one of the flattened cigarettes, lighting it and trying to think. But it was no good, my brain refused to function.

I looked about me. Jagged holes gaped in the airship's hull. Most of the gasbags had been ripped open and the helium lost. The wreckage covered a vast area of the mountainside. There was nowhere I looked which was not littered with it. And over it all moved thick ribbons of smoke from the volcano. The smoke stroked the broken bones of the ship, the smashed gondolas, the ruined engine nacelles, like the phantoms of the dead welcoming others into their ranks.

I got up and put out the cigarette with a stained, scratched boot. I coughed on the fumes and shivered with reaction and with cold. The slope was probably a thousand feet above sea-level. It was not surprising that the overloaded ship had crashed. Numbly I continued my search for survivors but at the end of two hours had found only corpses. What was still more horrifying was that many had actually survived the crash. As I searched I found little girls and boys who had been shot through the head or had their throats cut, young and old women butchered by parangs, men who had been decapitated. The bandits had been through the survivors systematically killing all those who for one reason or another had been unable or unwilling to walk. As the horror increased I was suddenly seized by nausea and stood with one hand leaning on a rock while I vomited again and again until all that came out of me were dry, retching coughs. Then I walked back to the main wreckage and found a blanket and a plastic container of water. I stripped off my useless lifejacket and wrapped myself in the blanket, stumbling up the mountainside until I was clear of the corpses. Then I slept.

* * *

awoke before dawn and was shivering. From somewhere below came a chilling howl which at first I mistook for that of a human being. Then I realized that the howl came from a wild dog hunting in the forest at the foot of the mountain. As dawn broke I went back to the wreck.

By now I had worked out roughly what had happened. Plainly the crash had been witnessed by one of the many rebel gangs who normally occupied these heights and, from time to time, would raid the Dutch towns and farmsteads below. Inspired by the support of both the Japanese and their more sophisticated nationalist countrymen, these rebels had recently grown bolder and had come to offer a serious threat to the colonists. Whether they called themselves bandits, pirates or "nationalists", all hated the whites in general and the Dutch in particular. They had captured the survivors probably as hostages or possibly to deliver to their Japanese friends in return for more guns or supplies. Possibly they might just want to take pleasure in killing them slowly. I couldn't be sure. But I did know that if they found me I should suffer the same fate and none of the prospects were pleasant.

There had been few weapons aboard the hospital ship and for all I was inclined to arm myself I did not bother to hunt among the dead for a gun. The rebels would probably have found any there were. Instead I rescued another plastic container of water, a box of rather stale sandwiches, discovered a kitbag of medical supplies which I shouldered and then, thoughtfully, for I knew I might sooner or later find myself in thick jungle, tugged a parang from the body of one of the very nurses who had restored me to health at Changi.

I stumbled away from the broken hulk of the aircraft, going down the mountain. My eyes stung and my throat felt clogged with sulphur.

I was still moving as if in a trance—moving, as it were, from one dream and into another. Nothing had seemed completely real since the first ships of the Japanese Air Fleet had been sighted in the skies over Singapore.

Yet for all that I went warily through the drifting smoke. I had no wish to be plunged into the nightmare of capture by the Malay bandits.

At last I emerged into hot sunshine, saw blue, calm sky above me and the rich, variegated greens of a forest below. I looked about for signs of the bandits and their captives but I could see nothing.

Beyond the forest was a faint line in the sky. It was the horizon of the sea. The airship had almost succeeded in crossing the island and would have done if the wind had not driven it against what I now saw was the highest mountain in the region. I would try for the ship's destination of Djogjakarta and pray that the city was still in Dutch hands. My best bet would be to cross the intervening land to the sea and then follow the beach more or less westward until I got to the town, or, with luck, find a road on which I could get a lift.

There was no point in trying to do anything for the captured survivors myself. Once in Djogjakarta I could tell the authorities what had happened and hope that Dutch hovergyros would go out with soldiers and save the people.

And so I began my journey to the sea.

It took three days, first through the thick jungle and out onto the plains until I came to the paddy fields which I had to wade through, making wide detours around villages in case the local peasants were, as was often the case, in league with the bandits.

It was an exhausting trip and I was half-starved by the time I saw the beach ahead, not an hour's march away. In some relief I began to wade through the last paddy, my ruined boots dragged at the clinging mud and then I stopped, hearing a familiar sound in the distance.

It was the drone of an airship's engines. I looked up and located the source. A silver flash in the sky.

Tears came into my eyes and my shoulders slumped as I realized my struggle was over. I was delivered. I started to yell and wave, though it was unlikely that the crew could even see me at that height, let alone distinguish me for a shipwrecked Englishman!

But the ship *was* coming down. It did seem to be looking for me. Perhaps a rescue ship from Surabaya? I cursed myself for not staying near the wreck where I might have been seen earlier. Up to my waist in water, surrounded by the neat rows of rice plants, I waved my parang and yelled still louder.

Then I saw the motif on the ship's hull and instantly I had plunged up to my neck among the plants, pulling them over my head.

The ship bore the red disc of the sun blazoned on its flanks. It was a vessel of the Imperial Japanese Air Fleet.

For a few moments the ship circled the area and then flew off towards the mountains. I waited until it had disappeared before daring to emerge from the water. I had become a timid creature in the past twenty-four hours.

More warily than ever I crept to the seashore until at last I lay exhausted in the shadow of the rock on a warm beach of black, volcanic sand against which beat the heavy white surf of the Indian Ocean.

The presence of the scout ship over Java was ominous. It meant that Japan felt strong enough to ignore Dutch neutrality. It could even mean that Japan, or the bandits who served her, had taken the island.

I wondered if there were now any point in my trying to reach Djogjakarta. I knew that the Japanese were not kind to their captives.

The sound of the surf seemed to grow louder and louder and more and more restful until soon the questions ceased to plague me as I stretched out on the soft sand and let my weary brain and body sink into sleep.

CHAPTER FIVE

The Price of Fishing Boats

At noon on the next day I saw the fishing village. It was a somewhat ramshackle collection of log and wattle huts of various sizes. All the huts were thatched with palm leaves and some had been raised on stilts. The dugouts, moored to rickety wooden jetties built out into the shallows, were primitive and hardly looked seaworthy. The huts were shaded by tall palms whose curving trunks and wide leaves appeared to offer greater shelter than the houses themselves.

I shrank back behind a hillock and deliberated for a few moments. There was a chance that the villagers were in league with either the Japanese or the bandits or both. Yet, for all I was desperate to get to safety, I was tired of hiding, I was dreadfully hungry, and had reached a point where I did not much care who those villagers were, or to whom they felt loyalty—just as long as they fed me something and let me lie down out of the glare of the sun.

I made my decision and plodded forward. I thought I knew the kind of white man these people would be most prepared to tolerate and feed.

I had reached the centre of the village before they began to emerge, first the adult men, then the women, then the children. They glowered at me. I smiled back, holding up my pack. "Medicine," I said, desperately trying to recall my vocabulary.

They all looked to me as if they could use what I had to offer.

A few villagers emerged from the general crowd. These all carried old guns, parangs and knives which, in spite of their age, looked pretty serviceable.

"Medicine," I said again.

There was a stirring from the back of the crowd. I heard words in an unfamiliar dialect. I prayed that some of them spoke Malay and that they would give me a chance to talk to them before they killed me. There was no question that my presence was resented.

An older man pushed his way through the armed villagers. He had bright, cunning eyes, and a calculating frown. He looked at my bag and uttered a couple of words in his dialect. I replied in Malay. This had to be the headman, for he was far better dressed than his fellows in a yellow-and-red silk sarong. There were sandals on his feet.

"*Belanda*?" he said. "Dutch?"

I shook my head. "*Inggeris*." I was not sure if he saw any difference between a Dutchman and an Englishman. But his brow cleared a little. He nodded.

"I have medicine." Carefully I enunciated the Malay words, for his dialect was not one with which I was familiar. "I can help your sick."

"Why do you come like this, without a boat or a car or a flying machine?"

"I was on a ship." I pointed out to sea. "It caught fire. I swam here. I wish to go to—to Bali. If you want me to cure your sick, you must pay me."

A slow smile crossed his lips. This made sense to him. I had come to bargain. Now he looked at me almost in relief.

"We have little money," he said. "The Dutch do not pay us for our fish now that the *Orang Djepang* war against them." He pointed up the coast towards Djogjakarta. "They fight."

I disguised my despair. So now there was no point in trying to reach the town. I would have to think of another plan.

"We have rice," said the headman. "We have fish. But no money."

I decided to continue with my original idea. If it worked I would be a little better off. "I want a boat. I will cure what sickness I can, but you must give me one of the boats with the engines."

The headman's eyes narrowed. The boats were their most valuable possessions. He sniffed and he frowned and he pursed his lips. Then he nodded. "You will stay with us until ten men fall ill and are cured and five women and five male children," he said, lowering his eyes.

I guessed that he was trying to hide any hint in his eyes that he might be getting the best of the bargain.

"Five men," I said.

"Ten men."

I spread my hands. "I agree."

And that was how I came to spend more weeks than I had planned in a remote and faintly hostile little Javanese fishing village, for the headman, of course, had tricked me.

The men proved disappointingly healthy and the women and children seemed constantly sick of minor complaints so that, with my limited medical knowledge, I treated many more people than had been called for in the original bargain, but I never seemed in sight of making up the male quota. The headman had realized at once that he was on to a good thing and it was soon evident that even when the men did fall sick they did not report to me but stuck to their usual methods of cure. At least two died while I was there. They were prepared to forego any attention from me so that I should continue treating the women and children.

For all that, I was scarcely angry. The routine was an anodyne to my weary brain and I lost myself in it. My awareness of any reality beyond the confines of the village grew steadily more vague. Chaos had come again to the outside world, but the day-to-day life of the village was the model of simple order and I might have lived my life there if the outside world had not, at last, intruded.

Looking back, I understand that it was inevitable, but I was surprised when it happened.

One morning I saw a cloud of dust in the distance. It seemed that the sand of the beach was being disturbed, but I could not distinguish the cause of the disturbance.

Then as the dust cloud came closer I realized what it meant and I ran to hide in the doorway of a hut.

The dust was thrown up by the tyres of military cars—big, square utilitarian things with heavy-duty steam turbines driving their massive wheels. And the military cars were crammed with Japanese soldiers. Almost certainly they had conquered the whole island by now and, as certainly, had heard some rumour of my presence in the village. They were coming to investigate.

It was at this point that I decided to sail for Australia. There was nowhere else to go.

Although I had failed to fulfill my original bargain with the headman, I still had the moral right to do what I did, for I had dealt fairly enough with the villagers. And I would leave what there was of my medical kit behind for them.

Taking only a petrol can full of water, I crept down to the shore, using a jetty as cover. Then I waded to one of the outboards and began to untie it. All the villagers were watching the oncoming cars and it was my only chance to escape. I started to push the boat slowly towards the open sea while the villagers ran about in excitement at the arrival of their new masters.

I was lucky. A current soon caught the dugout and carried it more rapidly away from the shore. At last the villagers saw me, realized what was happening just as the Japanese cars drew up in the village square. I was now some distance out and having trouble trying to climb into the dugout without upsetting it.

The villagers began to gesticulate and point towards me. With a heave I managed to get into the wildly rocking boat and tried to get the battered outboard going.

It fired after only three false starts. I adjusted the tiller and headed for the open sea, noticing with satisfaction that there were two spare cans of fuel stowed amidships.

I heard pistol shots, then rifle shots.

Then a machine-gun started up and bullets buzzed about my ears and struck the water all around me. I kept changing course and at one point did a complete circle and headed in the opposite direction to Darwin, my proposed destination, hoping that this would confuse them when they came to radio their headquarters and instruct them to send out airships and patrol boats to look for me.

The gunfire stopped for a moment. I looked back and saw the tiny figures of the villagers. They seemed to be kneeling before the Japanese.

Then the machine-gun started up again, but this time it did not fire out to sea.

* * *

A few hours later I began to think that the chances of pursuit had disappeared. I had sighted only one airship in the distance and soon it would be night. I had been lucky.

As I chugged out over the smooth and blazing mirror of the ocean, congratulating myself and with my thoughts increasingly turning to abstractions, I did not realize that the Japanese patrols must have been searching waters where I might logically be. It seems that I had already lost my bearings, in more senses than one.

As the burning days and the cold nights passed, I began to realize that I had no chance at all of reaching Australia, and I started to indulge in debates with my starving, thirsty self on the nature of life, the nature of death and the nature of what seemed to me a continuing struggle between Chaos and Order, with the former tending to come off rather better in the long run.

And it was this babbling and foolish wretch—once a practical and pragmatic soldier in a more orderly world—who eventually sighted Rowe Island and decided, reasonably, that it was nothing more than a splendidly detailed illusion.

CHAPTER SIX
The Mysterious Dempsey

Rove Island was discovered in 1615 by the British explorer Richard Rowe.

In 1887 it was found to contain formations of almost pure calcium and in 1888 was annexed by Great Britain. That year the first settlers arrived and by 1897 they had obtained a concession from the mother country to work the phosphate deposits. From being uninhabited before 1888, it had by the first third of this century achieved a population of more than two thousand, mainly Malay and Chinese miners who had come there to work for the Welland Rock Phosphate Mining Company, which was the island's sole industrial concern.

Rowe Island lies—or lay—in the Indian Ocean, 224 miles south, 8° east of Java Head and 259 miles north, 79° east of the Keeling Islands. It is 815 miles from the ruins of Singapore and 1,630 miles from what is left of Freemantle, Western Australia. Its European population used to number a hundred or so: the Official Representative and his staff; the manager and administrative staff of the Welland Rock Phosphate Mining Company; various private residents there for their health (Rowe Island was a very healthy place); a young lieutenant commanding the small garrison of Ghoorkas; some restaurant-, shop- and hotel-keepers; various missionaries and the airpark and dock officials. When I arrived most of these, of course, had already gone and neither airships nor steamers came to collect the island's only export.

The settlement had a mosque, a Buddhist temple, a Catholic church, a Methodist chapel and a mission hospital run by the Church of England. The hospital was staffed by a group of young Pakistani nursing nuns under the direction of a layman, Dr. Hira, a Sinhalese. The hospital's missionary and his wife had departed for Australia soon after the Destruction of Singapore.

It was in this hospital that I woke up and slowly realized Rowe Island was not, after all, an hallucination.

I was sore and my body stung all over, but I no longer felt thirsty, merely hungry. I lay between the rather rough linen sheets of what was evidently a white hospital bed. The walls were white and there was an ivory crucifix on the wall, a few tropical flowers stuck in a pot on the ledge by the partially opened window. I felt the urge to scratch, but discovered both hands were bandaged. I moved and my joints throbbed. I tried to sit upright, but fell back wearily. It was still hard to believe I was safe, after all. I had survived.

A little while later the door opened and in came a shy, beautiful Pakistani girl in a cream-coloured nun's habit. She nodded and smiled gravely at me, standing aside to admit a languid young Sinhalese whose portly frame was draped in an elegant white suit. Around his neck was a stethoscope on which the fingers of his right hand seemed to be playing a tune. His round, handsome face stared rather sardonically at me. He glanced at the watch on his plump wrist. "Not bad. Almost exactly on time."

My first attempt at speaking was not very successful. My second was better. "You," I said, "or me?"

"Both of us." He took a silver case from his pocket and

opened it, offering the cigarettes to me. I showed him my bandaged hands. He smiled apologetically. "The nurse will light it for you if you want one."

"Not now. Thanks."

He lit a cigarette for himself. "Well, you're on the mend I'm glad to say. We put you in this room because your shouting kept the other patients awake. You're an airshipman, are you?"

"I am," I said. "I was on an airship which crashed." I told him my name and what had happened to me. I asked where I was.

"I'm Dr. Hira. This is St. Charles' Hospital, Rowe Island." He smiled ironically. "I can see you've never heard of Rowe Island. Few have. Perhaps that's why the war hasn't touched us directly. Nobody passes this way either by air or by sea. In a few more months I wouldn't be surprised if we're the last outpost of civilization on the globe." He drew heavily on his cigarette and glanced out of the window at the harbour. The Pakistani nurse got extra pillows and helped me sit up.

"If you can call this civilization," said Hira. "Are you hungry?"

"Very."

"Good." Hira patted the shy nun on the shoulder. "Fetch the patient some soup, my dear."

When the nurse had gone, closing the door behind her, I gestured with my bandaged hands. "I thought this whole bloody place was a mirage, at first."

Hira shrugged. "Maybe it is. A pretty run-down dream, though. You survived Singapore, eh?"

"It's hard to believe it really happened," I said.

"It happened. We heard."

"So there's some communication with the outside world?"

"The mine people took all the decent equipment when they left. It was the news of Singapore that caused the evacuation. A needless panic as it turned out."

"I see. So there's no way of contacting, say, Darwin?"

"We've a radio which occasionally works. Hand-cranked thing."

"And those dhows are the only means of leaving the island. No ships of any kind?"

"Not any more, Mr. Bastable. The mine people scuttled our only steamer with some idea of stopping the island being used as a base for enemy shipping." Hira pointed out of the window at the harbour where the rusting superstructure of the wreck could still be seen.

"So I'm stuck here unless the radio can be made to work. You said it was 'hand-cranked'. Haven't you any proper power?"

"No more fuel. We use oil-lamps for lighting now."

"When is there a chance of my getting a message to Darwin?"

"That depends on the state of the radio and the state of Underwood, the operator. I'll ask someone to go up to the airpark tomorrow and see if Underwood is sober enough to work the radio. That's about the best I can do. Eager to get back into the fray, eh?"

I looked suspiciously at him, trying to detect irony in a face which now regarded me blandly.

"I've a duty," I said. "They'll need experienced airmen, after all."

"I'm sure they will. I must be off on my rounds now. See you soon, Mr. Bastable."

Hira raised the stethoscope in a kind of salute and left the room.

I sank back into the bed and sighed. An old radio and a drunken operator. I was pessimistic about my immediate chances of leaving Rowe Island.

* * *

A week went by and every day I grew stronger. I was making a splendid recovery from what had been a very serious case of exposure. But I also grew more and more impatient and plagued Dr. Hira with questions about the radio and the condition of the operator. The news initially brought back to the hospital had been bad. Shortly after I'd arrived Underwood had gone up on the mountain somewhere. He had taken a Chinese girl and a case of gin with him and he couldn't be found.

About ten days after I had awakened from my coma I stood by the window, wearing a rather ridiculous hospital dressing gown which was too short for me, talking to Hira, who had come in to give me the latest lack of news about Underwood. In the harbour there was a lot of confusion and noise. Since dawn groups of half-starved Malays had been moving along the jetty, packing their possessions into one of the fishing dhows. Apparently my appearance on Rowe Island had started something. They had realized that the mining company would not be back for a long while and they had decided to try to make it to Java, in spite of their having been warned of atrocities committed on their countrymen by the Japanese. I felt sorry for those Malays. The boat would probably sink before they got more than a few miles out. Miserably I looked back into the room at Hira.

"The government should be helping these people—flying in supplies or something. I wish that damned operator would turn up."

"I think the government has a lot of problems at the moment." Hira was sitting on my bed fiddling with his stethoscope. He spoke almost with satisfaction. "I don't know when we'll see Underwood. He often goes to earth like this. He's probably hiding out in one of the mines."

"I could have a try at working the radio myself," I said. "It would be better than this. I'm well enough to go out now. If you could find me a suit, perhaps…"

"I think we can discover something in your size. But Underwood has locked his office up. Always does. He likes to be indispensable. It keeps his credit good at the hotel."

"Which hotel?"

"Olmeijer's. The Royal Airpark Hotel on the edge of the airpark. It used to be the biggest. Now it's the only one. Olmeijer carries on running it from sentiment, I think."

"I'll take a stroll out there, anyway." I was curious to have a look at the island.

"Why not?" said Hira. "Get to know the place. After all, you could be here for some time." He seemed amused.

As I dressed in my borrowed suit, Hira took my place by the window. From the harbour came a babble of voices as the Malays readied the ship for the sea. He shook his head. "They'll drown themselves for certain."

"Won't anybody stop them?" I pulled on my jacket. The linen suit was a surprisingly good fit, as was the white shirt Hira had lent me. "Isn't there some sort of governor here? You mentioned someone…"

"Brigadier L.G.A. Nesbit is the Official Representative and has been since 1920." Hira shrugged. "He's eighty-seven and has been senile for at least ten years. I think that's why he decided to stay when the big exodus was on. His staff now consists of a valet as old as himself and a Bengali secretary who spends his whole time making endless inventories and who hasn't, apparently, left his office since the war began. There is, of course, young Lieutenant Begg, who commands our local military. I don't think Begg will be sorry to see a few of his troubles going."

"The Malays are a problem, eh?" I tried on one of the panama hats lying on the bed. It was a good fit, too.

Hira gestured wearily. "There are a thousand Malays and Chinese here at least. The Malays are in the main Moslems and the Chinese are chiefly Buddhists or Christians. They are, when they have nothing better to do, highly critical of the other's way of life. And they have nothing better to do—their work went when the mine closed and now they're living off the land and sea as best they can."

"Poor bastards," I said.

Hira gave a peculiar smile. "I wonder if you'll say that when they turn on the whites. They will, you know, quite soon. Presently they hate each other more than they hate Europeans, but it will take just one excuse for them to begin a general massacre. We'll all go, then. Technically, you see, the sisters and myself are regarded as Europeans."

"And you're prepared to stay until that happens?"

"Should I go back to Ceylon and care for our Japanese conquerors?"

"You could go to Australia or even England. There must be need of doctors everywhere."

"I should have made it plain." Hira opened the door for me. "I have a couple of principles. One of them is that I refuse to work for Europeans. It's the reason I came to Rowe Island in the first place. Until the evacuation this hospital was for coloured people only, Mr. Bastable."

As I left the hospital I adjusted my hat and paused to watch the dhow easing its way past the wreck of the steamer. Every inch of its deck was covered with brown-skinned men, women and children. It brought back the terrible image of the doomed hospital ship and I could hardly bear to think what would become of them all. Slowly I started to walk along the weed-grown quay, beside deserted hotels, offices and warehouses outside which were parked the useless cars, lorries and buses.

A few disconsolate Malays were dragging their bundles back down the jetty, having failed to squeeze themselves aboard the boat. The lucky ones, I thought.

I reached a corner and turned into a narrow, silent side street lined with grey-and-brown featureless workers' houses and a few boarded-up shops. The street rose quite steeply and I realized how weak I still was, for I had to labour the last few paces until I reached a small square dominated by a battered statue of Edward VIII which somewhat incongruously decorated a dried-up ornamental fountain. The concrete bowl of the fountain was full of empty bottles, torn newspapers and other, less savoury, refuse. There were a few Chinese children playing around it while their mothers sat blank-faced in their doorways, staring into space. Gratefully, I sat on the edge of the fountain's bowl, ignoring the smell which came from it and smiling at the undernourished children. They at once stopped playing and looked warily up at me.

"*Tso sun*," I said gravely, using Cantonese. "Good morning."

Not one of them replied. A bit nonplussed, I wished I had something to offer them. Some sweets, perhaps, for money was worthless on Rowe Island.

I removed my hat and wiped my forehead. It was growing very hot and I had become wary of the sun. I had better get on to the hotel while I could.

Then I heard the sound of hoof beats and turned in astonishment to see a rider enter the square. He looked distinctly out of place as he sat stiff-backed and arrogant in the saddle of his well-groomed cob. A tall, fair-haired Englishman of about thirty, he wore a gleaming white coat and jodhpurs with his military insignia on the jacket. His boots, belt, shoulder strap and holster were as highly polished as the badge on his solar topee. He saw me at once, but pretended that he hadn't. He stroked his blond moustache with his baton and brought his horse to a halt on the other side of the square.

I looked around at the empty, silent windows, wondering what he could be doing here.

"Get these children out of the way, sergeant!" His voice was sharp, commanding.

At this order six crisply turned-out little Ghoorkas led by a sergeant emerged from another side street and waved the children back with their rifles. Their bayonets were fixed. They wore dark green uniforms with scarlet facings and they had their long, curved knives at their belts. The women needed no warnings but dragged the children inside and slammed their doors. Now I was the only civilian in the square.

"What's going on here, lieutenant?" I asked.

The lieutenant turned cold, blue eyes on me. "I would suggest, sir, that you get away from here at once. It's a police matter. There could be trouble."

There seemed to be no point in arguing. I humoured him instead. "Thank you, lieutenant." I walked across the square but remained in the shadows of a side street, peering curiously at what was going on.

Now the young officer dismounted and ordered his sergeant to enter one of the houses. The Ghoorkas rushed in and the lieutenant followed behind.

I watched in puzzlement, not knowing what to make of the scene at all. There was dead silence in the square for a little while, then a horrible babble of screams and yells issued from the house. I heard a woman shouting in Cantonese. There were a couple of shots and then the raised voice of the officer giving a series of orders. Another scream—a man's this time—then out into the street poured a score of coolies. They were staggering and screwing their eyes up against the sunlight. Every one of them was dazed and scared stiff.

There came another shot from inside the house and then more shouting. The coolies outside began to scatter, some rushing into nearby doorways, others running off down towards the harbour. A further series of commands came from the officer and then a terrible wailing, the sound of flesh being struck, presumably with rifle butts.

Appalled, I was about to step forward when a panic-stricken coolie burst from the house, hesitated, glanced around wildly holding a bleeding hand, then ran in my direction. I stepped aside to let him pass and he fled around a corner and vanished. But I had seen his pupils. The man had been drugged. Now I understood. The soldiers were raiding some sort of local opium den.

Hearing a moan, I re-entered the square and saw that one of the opium smokers had fallen to the flagstones. He had been stabbed badly with a bayonet in his shoulder. I knelt beside him, tore back his shirt and did my best to stop the flow of blood while he stared at me in terror, small moans escaping his lips.

Boots tramped from the house.

"Good God, man, what are you doing?"

I looked up to see the lieutenant striding from the house. He looked pretty pleased with himself.

"This chap's been stabbed by one of your soldiers," I said harshly. "I'm trying to help him. Was there any need to—"

The lieutenant glanced contemptuously at the coolie. "Doubtless he tried to kill someone. Crazed by opium—they all are. His own people will look after him. We're trying to teach them a lesson, after all."

With strips of the man's shirt I bandaged up the wound as best I could. He tried to speak and then fainted. Helplessly, I tried to lift him, but it was impossible.

Now the Ghoorkas emerged holding three terrified Chinese in black-and-red smocks; two men and a woman, all badly bruised and probably the proprietors of the den.

The lieutenant's baton stabbed in their direction. He raised his head and spoke to the empty windows and doors. "Now no more opium! You savvy! Opium bad! These people bad! Go to prison. We lock up long time! Savvy?"

Angrily he tapped his riding boot with his baton. He glared at me and opened his mouth to speak.

"I'm going to try to get this chap to the hospital," I said. "Can somebody give me a hand?"

The officer took the reins of his horse and looked from me to his soldiers who held their miserable prisoners much more firmly than was necessary.

"One of your men—" I began.

The lieutenant remounted. "I told you, sir. His own people will look after him. You obviously don't understand the conditions on this island. There's a dreadful opium problem. It's increasing daily. They grow the poppies rather than food. I…"

"What else have the bastards got to live for, Begg?" A tired drawl came from the shadowy doorway of the raided house. An English voice.

Lieutenant Begg turned in his saddle and shook his baton at the unseen speaker. "You stay out of this. You're lucky we didn't arrest you, too."

A figure emerged into the sunlight. Dressed in a dirty, faded European suit and a frayed native shirt, he was barefooted, unshaven, emaciated and plainly under the influence of opium. I knew the signs well enough, for I had once been slave to the drug's consolations. I could not make out his age, but the voice was of quite a young man from the upper middle class.

"I'd have thought you'd be ashamed…" Begg's face was full of disgust.

"Who are you to deny them their only pleasure, Begg?" drawled the newcomer reasonably. "Let them alone, for God's sake."

Lieutenant Begg wheeled his trim cob about and shouted an order to his men. "All right, quick march." He trotted away without answering the decrepit Englishman.

I watched them go, the Ghoorkas dragging their frightened prisoners back the way they had come.

The Englishman shrugged and turned to re-enter the house.

"Just a minute," I called. "I must try to get this chap to the hospital. He's half-dead. Could you give me a hand?"

The man leaned wearily against the door frame. "He'd be better off with his ancestors, believe me."

"A moment ago you were defending these people."

"Not defending them, old boy. I'm a fatalist, you see. I told Begg to let them alone. And I tell you the same. What's the point? He'll die soon enough."

But he left the doorway and shuffled into the square, blinking in the sunshine. "Who are you, anyway?"

"I'm an airshipman. I got here a week or so ago."

"Ah, the shipwrecked mariner. They were talking about you up at the hotel. All right, I'll help you with him, for what it's worth."

The opium-drunk Englishman was no stronger than I was, but together we managed to carry the coolie down the street and along the quay until we reached the hospital.

After a couple of nuns had been called and had taken the wounded man away, I stood panting in the lobby, staring curiously at my helper. "Thanks."

He smiled slowly. "Think nothing of it. Nothing at all. Cheerio."

He raised his hand in a sort of ironic salute and then went out. He had gone before Dr. Hira came down the stairs into the lobby.

"Who was that chap?" I asked Hira, describing the wretched Englishman.

Hira recognized the description. He fiddled with his stethoscope. "A castaway, like yourself. He arrived in the airship which came to take off the mine people. He chose to stay on Rowe Island. I don't know why. It meant they could take one more passenger so they didn't argue. They call him The Captain sometimes, up at the hotel. Supposed to have been the commander of a merchant airship which crashed in China before the war. A bit of a mystery."

"Begg doesn't like him."

Hira laughed softly. "No, Begg wouldn't. Captain Dempsey lets the side down, eh? Begg's for the Europeans keeping up appearances at all costs."

"Begg certainly works hard." I wiped a spot of blood off my sleeve.

"I don't think he ever sleeps. His wife left with the mine people, you know…" Hira glanced at his watch. "Well, it's almost lunchtime. Fish and rice, as usual, but I've managed to get a couple of bottles of beer, if you'd…"

"No thanks," I said. "I think I'll head up to the hotel again."

CHAPTER SEVEN
Dead Man

The port where I was staying was the only real town on the island. It was called New Birmingham. Its buildings were clustered close together near the waterfront and were several storeys high. As they wandered up the slopes they drew apart as if fastidious of each other's squalor and grew smaller until the houses near the top were little more than isolated shanties erected in shallow hollows in the hillside.

Above the shanty district the hill leveled out for a while and became a small plateau on which the airpark had been built. Olmeijer's hotel stood on the edge of the airpark, which was now overgrown and desolate. I wondered if young Lieutenant Begg would have approved of the hotel, for it had certainly made an attempt to "keep up appearances". Its big gilt sign was brightly polished and its splendid wooden Gothic exteriors had recently been given a fresh coat of white paint. It looked out of place in its surroundings.

The airpark was dominated by the rusting airship mast erected in its centre. To one side of the park was a single airship hangar, its grey paint peeling, and beside it a pole at which drooped a torn and filthy windsock. Near the pole stood, like the skeletons of large, unearthly insects, the remains of two hovergyros which had been stripped of most of their essential parts. On the other side of the hangar was the shell of a light monoplane, probably the property of some long-gone sportsman, which had been similarly dismembered. The island seemed to be populated by a variety of wrecks, I thought. It seemed to be feeding off corpses, including, as in Begg's case, the corpses of dead ideas.

After a glance towards the abandoned administration and control buildings to assure myself that they were uninhabited, I made for the hotel.

Pushing open a pair of well-oiled double doors, I walked into the lobby. It was clean, scrubbed, polished and cool. A Malay houseboy was operating the cords of a big punka attached to the ceiling. It fanned air into my face as I entered. I was grateful for this after the heat outside but amused by the fresh incongruity. I nodded to the Malay, who didn't seem to notice me and, seeing no one at the desk, strolled into the adjacent bar.

In the shady gloom were two men. One sat in his shirtsleeves behind the bar reading a book while the other sat drinking a gin fizz in the far corner near French windows opening onto a verandah. Beyond the windows I could see the airpark and beyond the airpark the slopes of the mountain, covered in thick forest.

As I seated myself on a stool by the bar the man behind it put down his book and looked at me in some surprise. He was very fat and his big, red face was beaded with sweat. His rolled-up sleeves revealed a variety of tattoos of the more restrained kind. There were several gold rings on his thick fingers. He spoke in a deep, guttural accent.

"What can I do for you?"

I began apologetically, "I'm afraid I brought no money, so…"

The fat man's face broke into a broad smile. "Ja! No money!

That's too bad!" He shook with laughter for a moment. "Now, what will you drink. I'll put it on the slate, eh?"

"Very good of you. I'll have a brandy." I introduced myself. "Are you the hotel's proprietor?"

"Ja. I am Olmeijer, certainly." He seemed inordinately proud of the fact. He took a large ledger from under the counter, selected a fresh page and entered my name at the top. "Your account," he said. "When things are better, you can pay me." He turned to take down a bottle of cognac.

"You've a chap called Underwood staying here, I believe?" I said.

"Underwood, certainly." He put a large brandy on the bar. "Twenty cents. On the slate." He made an entry in the ledger and replaced it out of sight.

It was good brandy. Perhaps it tasted even better for being the first drink I had had since Singapore. I savoured it.

"But Underwood," said Olmeijer with a wink and a jerk of his thumb, "has gone up the mountain."

"And you've no idea when he'll be back."

I heard one of the wicker chairs scrape on the polished floor, then footsteps approached me. I turned. It was the man who had been sitting near the window. He held his empty glass in his hand.

"Underwood will be back when the gin he borrowed from Mr. Olmeijer runs out."

He was a thin, heavily tanned man in his fifties, wearing a khaki bush shirt and white shorts. He had a small, greying moustache and his blue eyes seemed to have a permanent hint of ironic humour in them. "My name's Nye," he said as he joined me at the bar. "You must be the airship chap they found in the dugout. Singapore, eh? Must have been awful."

Nye told me he'd been left behind to protect the interests of the Welland Rock Phosphate Mining Company while the rest of the white employees went back to England or Australia. He was keen to hear about the attack on Singapore. Briefly, for the memory was still hard to bear, I told him what had happened.

"I still can't believe it," I concluded. "There was a peace treaty."

He smiled bitterly and sipped his drink. "Everyone had a peace treaty, didn't they? We'd abolished war, hadn't we? But human nature being what it is…" He looked up at the rows of bottles in front of him. "Bloody Japs. I knew they'd start something sooner or later. Greedy bastards!"

"The Japanese would not have blown up their own—" began Olmeijer. Nye interrupted him with a sharp laugh.

"I don't know how that city got blown up, but it was the excuse everybody needed to start scrapping." He tilted his glass to his lips. "I suppose we'll never know how it happened or who did it. But that's not the point. They'd have been fighting by now even if it hadn't happened."

"I wish you were right!"

I recognized the new voice and turned to see Dempsey walking wearily into the bar. He nodded to me and Nye and placed a dirty hand on the counter. "Large scotch please, Olmeijer."

The Dutchman didn't seem pleased to see his latest customer, but he poured the drink and carefully wrote the cost down in his ledger.

There was an embarrassed pause. For all he had interrupted our conversation, Dempsey apparently wasn't prepared to amplify his remark.

"Afternoon, Dempsey," I said.

He smiled faintly and rubbed at his unshaven chin. "Hello, Bastable. Moving in?"

"I was looking for Underwood."

He took a long pull at his drink. "There's a lot of people looking for Underwood," he said mysteriously.

"What do you mean?"

He shook his head. "Nothing."

"Another drink, Bastable?" said Nye. "Have this one on me." And then, as if with a slight effort. "You, Dempsey?"

"Thanks." Dempsey finished his drink and put his glass back on the bar. Olmeijer poured another gin, another brandy, another scotch.

Nye took a case of cheroots from his shirt pocket and offered them around. Olmeijer and Dempsey accepted, but I refused. "What did you mean, just then?" Nye asked Dempsey. "You don't care about all this, surely? I thought you were the chap so full of oriental fatalism."

Dempsey turned away. For a moment his dead eyes had seemed to burn with a terrible misery. He took his glass to a nearby table and sat down. "That's me," he said.

But Nye wouldn't let it go. "You weren't in Japan when the bombing started, were you?"

Dempsey shook his head. "No, China." I noticed that his hands were shaking as he lifted his glass to his mouth and he seemed to be muttering something under his breath. I thought I heard the words "God forgive me". He finished the drink quickly, got up and shambled towards the door. "Thanks, Nye. See you later."

His wasted body disappeared through the doors and I saw him begin to climb the flight of wooden stairs which led up from the lobby.

Nye raised his eyebrows in a quizzical look. He shrugged. "I think Dempsey has become what we used to call an 'island case'. We had a few of them going native, in the old days, or taking up opium, like him. The stuff's killing him, of course, and he knows it. He'll be dead within six months, I shouldn't wonder."

"I'd have given him longer than that," I said feelingly. "I've known opium smokers who live to a ripe old age."

Nye drew on his cheroot. "It's not just the opium, is it? I mean, there's such a thing as a *will* to die. You know that as well as I do."

I nodded soberly. I had encountered my own share of such desires.

"I wonder what did it," Nye mused. "A woman, perhaps. He was an airshipman, you know. Perhaps he lost his ship, or deserted her or something?"

Olmeijer grunted and looked up from his book. "He's just a weak man. Just weak, that's all."

"Could be." I got up. "I think I'll head back now. Mind if I come up tomorrow? I'd like to be here when Underwood returns."

"See you tomorrow." Nye lifted his hand in a salute. "I wish you the best of luck, Bastable."

That night I dined on fish and fruit with Hira. I told him about my conversation at the hotel and my second encounter with Dempsey. His earlier remark had aroused my curiosity and I asked Hira if he knew anything at all of Dempsey's reasons for coming to the island.

Hira could add little about the opium eater. "All I know is that he was in better condition when he arrived than he is now. I don't have much to do with the European community, as you may have noticed." He looked sardonically at me. "Englishmen often start acting strangely when they've been out East a few years. Maybe they feel guilty about exploiting us, eh?"

I refused to rise to this and we completed our meal in relative silence.

After dinner we sat back in our chairs and smoked, discussing the health of the coolie I had found. Hira told me he was recovering reasonably quickly. I was just about to go up to bed when the door opened suddenly and a nun rushed into Hira's room. "Doctor—quickly—it is Underwood!" Her face was full of anxiety. "He has been attacked. I think he is dying."

We hurried downstairs to the little entrance hall of the hospital. In the light from the oil lamp I saw Olmeijer and Nye standing there. Their faces were pale and tense and they were staring helplessly down at something which lay on an improvised stretcher they had placed on the floor. They must have carried it all the way from the hotel.

Hira crouched down and inspected the man on the stretcher. "My God!" he said.

Nye addressed me. "He was dumped on the steps of the hotel about an hour ago. I think some Chinaman objected to his wife or maybe his daughter running off with Underwood. I don't know." Grimly he wiped his face with his handkerchief. "This couldn't have happened before the bloody war…"

I gagged as I got a good look at the battered mess of flesh on the stretcher. "Poor devil!"

Hira straightened up and looked significantly at me. There was no hope for Underwood. He turned to Nye and Olmeijer. "Can you take the stretcher up to the ward, please?"

I followed as the two men picked up the stretcher and staggered as they climbed the short flight of steps to the ward. With the nurses, I helped get him onto the bed, but it was plain that virtually every bone in his body had been broken. He was scarcely recognizable as a human being. They had taken their time in beating him up and he couldn't last long.

Hira began to fill a hypodermic. The beaten man's eyes opened and he saw us. His lips moved.

I bent to listen.

"Bloody Chinks… bloody woman… done for me. Found us in the mine… The sheets… Oh, God… The bloody clubs…"

Hira gave him a hefty injection. "Cocaine," he said to me. "It's about all we have now."

I looked at the next bed and saw the coolie I had rescued

staring at Underwood with an expression of quiet satisfaction.

"This couldn't be some sort of retaliation, could it?" I asked Hira.

"Who knows?" Hira looked down at the Australian as the man's eyes glazed and closed again.

Nye put his fist to his lips and cleared his throat. "I wonder if somebody ought to tell Nesbit…" He looked at Underwood and pursed his lips. "There'll be hell to pay when Begg hears about this."

Hira seemed almost amused. "It could mean the end."

Thoughtfully, Olmeijer rubbed at his neck. "Need Begg be told?"

"The man has been attacked," I said. "A couple of hours or so and it will be murder. He can't last the night."

"If Begg goes on the rampage, old boy, we all stand a chance of being murdered," Nye pointed out. "Begg will anger the Malays and Chinese so much they're bound to turn on us. These aren't the old days. What do you think a dozen bloody Ghoorkas can do against a thousand coolies?"

There was a glint of malice in Hira's eyes. "So you don't want me to report this to the Official Representative, gentlemen?"

"Better not," said Nye. "We'll all keep mum, eh?"

I watched the nurse cleaning the blood from Underwood's body. The cocaine had knocked him out completely. I walked to the door of the ward and lit a cigarette, watching the mosquitoes and the moths fluttering around the oil lamp in the lobby. From beyond the open door came the sound of the sea striking the stones of the quay. It no longer seemed peaceful. Instead the silence had become ominous. As the other three men joined me I inclined my head.

"Very well," I said. "I'll say nothing."

* * *

ext morning New Birmingham was deathly quiet. I walked through empty streets. I felt I was watched by a thousand pairs of eyes as I made my way up to the airpark.

I did not call in at the hotel. There was no point now in hoping to see Underwood there. He had died in the night at the hospital. I carried on past it and stood by one of the ruined hovergyros, kicking at a broken rotor which lay on the weed-grown concrete beside the machine. From the forest behind me came the sounds of dawn. At this hour some of the nocturnal animals were still about and the diurnal inhabitants were beginning to wake. Hornbills, cockatoos, fairy bluebirds and doves fluttered among the trees, filling the air with song and with colour. They seemed to be celebrating something, perhaps the end of the human occupation of the island. The air was rich with the stink of the forest, of animal spoor and rotting tree trunks. I heard the chatter of gibbons and saw tiny shrews skipping along branches heavy with dew. On the wall of the hangar the beady eyes of lizards regarded me coldly as if I had no business to be there.

I turned towards what had been the main control building where the murdered man had locked up his wireless apparatus before going off on what was to prove his final orgy.

The whole building had been sealed before the airship personnel had left. The windows on all three storeys had been covered by steel shutters and it would take special tools and a lot of hard work to get even one of them down. All the doors were locked and barred and I could see where various attempts to open them had failed.

I walked round and round the concrete building, pushing uselessly at the shutters and rattling the handles of the doors. The chirring sounds from the forest seemed to mock my helplessness and at length I stopped by a door which had evidently been in recent use, tried the handle once more, then leaned against the frame, looking back across the deserted park, with its broken bones of flying machines and its rusting mast, at the spruce hotel beyond. The sun glinted on Olmeijer's gilded sign: ROYAL AIRPARK HOTEL, it said, THE ISLAND'S BEST.

A little later someone came out through the French windows leading from the bar and stood on the verandah. Then they saw me and began to walk slowly through the tall grass towards me.

I recognized the figure and I frowned. What could he want?

CHAPTER EIGHT
The Message

It was Dempsey. of course. He had shaved and put on a suit slightly cleaner than the one he had worn on the previous day, but he wore the same tattered native shirt underneath it. By the pupils of his eyes I saw he had not yet had his first pipe of opium.

He shuffled towards me, coughing on the comparatively cold air of the early morning. "I heard about Underwood," he said. He crossed the cracked concrete and stood looking at me.

I offered him a cigarette which he accepted, fumbling it from my case and trembling slightly as I lit it for him.

"You knew the Chinese were after Underwood, didn't you?" I said. "That's what you meant yesterday when you said a lot of people were looking for him."

"Yesterday? I don't remember." He puffed on the cigarette, drawing the smoke deep into his lungs.

"You might have saved him, Dempsey, if you'd warned someone at the time."

He straightened up a little and he seemed amused as he glanced towards the forest. "On the other hand I might have done everyone else more harm. It's a bit of a luxury, a social conscience, isn't it, Bastable?" He felt in his pocket. "I came to give you this. I found it on the steps." He held out a Yale key. "Must have fallen from Underwood's pocket when they dumped him."

I hesitated before accepting the key. Then I turned and tried it in the lock. The wards clicked back and the door swung open. The interior smelled of stale liquor and burnt rubber.

"All that's left of Underwood is his stink," said Dempsey. "Now you're going to try to wireless for help, I suppose."

"I'll try," I said. "If I can get through to Darwin I'll ask them to reroute the first available airship to pick me up—and anyone else who wants to leave the island."

"Better tell them it's an emergency." Dempsey waved his hand in the general direction of the town. "Make no bones about it. There are half a dozen excuses for an uprising now. Begg finding out about Underwood will be just one more. The Chinese are in a mood to slaughter all the Malays and if the whites interfere, they'll probably get together and kill us first. It's true." A ghost of a smile appeared on his lips. "I know. I'm in rather closer touch with the natives than most, after all. Underwood was just a beginning."

I nodded. "All right. I'll tell Darwin."

"You know how to work the wireless?"

"I've had some training…"

Dempsey followed me into the gloomy interior of the office. It was a filthy litter of empty beer cans, bottles and bits of broken wireless equipment. He pulled back the shutters and light came through the dusty windows. I saw what could only be the wireless set in one corner and I picked my way across the floor towards it.

Dempsey showed me the pedals underneath the bench. I sat down and put my feet on them. They turned slowly at first and then more easily.

Dempsey inspected the set. "Seems to be warming up," he said. He began to fiddle with the dials. There was a faint crackle from the phones. He picked them up and listened, shaking his head. "Valve trouble, probably. You'd better let me have a go."

I rose and Dempsey sat down in the chair. After a while he found a screwdriver and took part of the casing off the set. "It's the valves, all right," he said. "There should be a box of spares behind you on the other bench. Could you bring it over?"

I found the box and placed it beside him as he continued to work.

"Did you learn about radios on airships?" I asked him.

He tightened his mouth and went on with the job.

"How did you happen to turn up here?" I said, my curiosity overcoming my tact.

"None of your bloody business, Bastable. There, that should do it." He screwed in the last valve and began pedaling, but then he fell back in the chair coughing. "Too bloody weak," he said. "You'd better do the pumping, if you wouldn't mind…" He lapsed into another fit of coughing as he got up and I replaced him.

While I pedaled, he twisted the dials again until we heard a faint voice coming through the earphones. Dempsey settled the headset over his ears and adjusted the microphone. "Hello, Darwin. This is Rowe Island. Over." He turned a knob.

He flipped a toggle switch and spoke impatiently into the mike. "No, I'm sorry, I don't know our bloody call sign. Our operator's been killed as a matter of fact. No, we're not a military base. This is Rowe Island in the Indian Ocean and the civilian population is in danger."

While I continued to pedal the generator, Dempsey told Darwin our situation. There was some confusion, a wait of nearly twenty minutes while the operator checked with his superiors, some more confusion over the location of the island and then at last Dempsey leaned back and sighed. "Thank you, Darwin."

As he stripped off the headset he glanced down at me. "You're lucky. They'll have one of their patrol ships over here in a day or two—if it hasn't been shot down. You'd better tell the others to pack their bags and be ready."

"I'm very grateful, Dempsey," I said. "I don't think I'd have had a chance of getting through if it hadn't been for you."

The problems with the wireless had exhausted him. He got up and began to rummage around in the office until he found an almost full bottle of rum. He opened it, took a long drink, then offered it to me.

I accepted the bottle and sipped the rum, gasping. It was raw stuff. I handed it back and watched with a certain amount of respect as he finished it.

We left the office and began to walk across the airpark. As we approached the mast he paused and looked up through the girders. The passenger lift was at the top of the mast, presumably left there by the last hasty group to go aboard the ship when it had taken the bulk of the Europeans off the island. "This won't be any good," he said. "Nobody to work it, even if it was in decent condition. The ship will have to come right down. It's going to be a problem. Everybody will have to muck in."

"Will you help me?"

"If I'm conscious."

"I heard you commanded an airship once," I said.

Then I regretted my curiosity for a peculiar look of pained amusement came over his face. "Yes. Yes, I did. For a very short time."

I dropped it. "Let me get you a drink," I said.

Olmeijer was in his usual spot at the bar, reading his book. Nye was not there. The Dutchman looked up and nodded to us. He made no mention of the previous night's business and I didn't bring it up. I told him that we had managed to get through to Darwin and that they were sending an airship. He seemed unimpressed. I think he enjoyed his role as the last hotelier on the island. He would rather have customers who couldn't pay than no customers at all. Dempsey and I took our drinks to one of the tables near the window.

"You've been a great help, Dempsey," I said.

Cynically he stared at me over the rim of his glass. "Am I helping? I may be doing you a disservice. Do you really want to go back to all that?"

"I think it's my duty."

"Duty? To support the last vestiges of a discredited imperialism?"

It was the first time I had heard him utter anything like a political opinion. I was surprised. He sounded like a bit of a Red, I thought. I could think of no answer which wouldn't have been impolite.

He downed the rest of his scotch and stared out over the airpark, speaking as if to himself. "It's all a question of power and rarely a question of justice." He looked sharply at me. "Don't patronize me, Bastable. I don't need your kindness, thanks. If you knew…" He broke off. "Another?"

I watched Dempsey walk unsteadily to the bar and then get fresh drinks. He brought them back almost reluctantly.

"I'm sorry," I said. "It's just—well, you seem to have a lot on your mind. I thought a sympathetic ear…"

There was a very strange look in his eyes now. "Sympathetic? I wonder how sympathetic you would stay if I told you what was really on my mind. There's a war taking place, Bastable. I heard you speculating yesterday about how it started. I know how the war started. I know who started it, too. It was a bloody accident."

I restrained my exclamation of astonishment and waited to hear more, but Dempsey leaned back in the wicker chair and closed his eyes, his lips moving as he spoke to himself.

I went to get him another drink, but he was already asleep when I returned. I let him sleep and joined Olmeijer at the bar.

Shortly afterwards Nye came in. He looked tired, as if he had not been to bed since I had seen him.

"Give me a triple gin, Olmeijer, quick. Morning, Bastable. I don't advise you to go back through the town alone. There's a lot of trouble. Big gangs of Malays and Chinese fighting each other. Arson, rape and bloody murder all over the place."

"Has Begg found out about…?"

"Not yet, but pretty well everyone else knows. He'll hear soon. The Chinese managed to steal a Malay boat last night and buggered off with it—probably poor Underwood's murderers making their getaway. The Malays roughed up some Chinese families. The Chinese retaliated. I think we're in very hot water this time."

I told him about the wireless message to Darwin and the probability of a ship coming. He looked more than relieved. "You'd better send one of your chaps into New Brum, Olmeijer. Tell him to let everyone know—to get up here as fast as possible."

Grumbling, Olmeijer rolled off to find a servant.

Nye walked round to the other side of the bar. "I think another drink is called for—on the house. Bastable?" I nodded. "Dempsey?"

I saw that Dempsey had woken up and was making for the door. He shook his head and said with a tight, crooked smile, "I've some business in town. Cheerio."

"It's dangerous," I said.

"I'll be all right. Hope to see you later, Bastable."

We watched him leave.

"Poor bastard," said Nye. He shuddered and downed his gin.

CHAPTER NINE

Hopes of Salvation

Begg came up to the hotel in the afternoon and asked suspiciously after Underwood. We said that we had heard he'd had some sort of accident. He didn't believe us, of course, but he had his hands full in the town and couldn't wait to question us further. He'd escorted some clergymen to the hotel and some Chinese nuns from the Catholic mission. They sat huddled in the far corner of the bar and didn't talk much to us. Nesbit's secretary, a round-faced, anxious Bengali, had come with Begg and he remained almost constantly by the window, looking out as if he expected the airship to arrive at any minute. I asked Begg about Dempsey and the soldier glowered at me, muttering that Dempsey had been seen with some of the Chinese "rebels" and might find himself in real trouble with the authorities if he wasn't careful. I also learned that Hira had decided to stay on at the hospital along with most of his nuns.

By that evening a few more people had drifted up, including two Irish priests who joined the others in the corner. Olmeijer seemed delighted to have so many new guests and rushed around seeing that rooms were prepared for them. Even I received a room on the second floor.

Begg returned looking tired and angry. His normally neat uniform was dusty and he had a bruise over his right eye. He seemed to be blaming Nye and me for his problems and wouldn't speak to us at all on this second visit. He had brought us three of his twelve-man army for protection. The rest were remaining in the town to "keep order", though from the noise below there was precious little of that, and to protect the Official Representative's residence, for Brigadier Nesbit, it emerged, had elected to stay, along with his valet.

Begg returned a little later. He was alone and as stiff-backed as ever as he guided his horse down the hill and disappeared into the darkness and the cacophony below. I don't believe he was seen alive again.

By midnight the ladies and gentlemen of the cloth had all gone to bed and Nye, Olmeijer and myself were in our usual places at the bar while the little Bengali paced back and forth beside the windows.

Even Nye seemed a trifle nervous and once he expressed the belief that we "might not quite last out". Then he, too, went to bed and the Bengali followed him. Olmeijer had his big account book open on the bar and for a while seemed cheerfully engrossed in his arithmetic before closing the book with a crash, nodding goodnight to me, and heaving his huge bulk away to his own quarters.

Now, save for the Ghoorkas on guard outside, I was the only one up. I felt exhausted but not particularly sleepy. I decided to go outside and see if I could detect any activity in the town.

As I entered the lobby I heard voices by the main entrance. I peered out, but the oil lamp wasn't bright enough to show me anything. I opened the door. One of the Ghoorka guards was shouting at a man I could dimly see in the moonlight. The

Ghoorka gestured with his bayoneted rifle and the man turned away. For a moment I saw his face in the faint glow from the lamp in the lobby. I pushed past the soldier and hurried outside.

"Dempsey? Is that you?"

He looked back. His shoulders were bowed and his jacket had been ripped. His face was deathly pale, his eyelids almost closed. "Hello, Bastable." The speech was slurred. "Thought this was my hotel."

"It is." I went towards him and took a limp arm. "Come inside."

The Ghoorkas made no attempt to stop us as I led Dempsey into Olmeijer's. The man was staggering and shivering. A dry retching noise came from his throat. He was gripping something tightly in his right hand. There was no point in questioning him and I did my best to get him up the stairs and along the passage to his room.

The door was unlocked. I half-carried Dempsey in, let him sit on the bed while I lit the oil lamp.

The light revealed a room which was surprisingly neat. The bed was made up and there was no litter. In fact, the room was completely impersonal. I got Dempsey onto the bed and he stretched out with a sigh. The shivering came in brief spasms now. He blinked and looked up at me as I took his pulse. "Thank you very much, Bastable," he said. "I thought I might have a word with you."

"You're in bad shape," I said. "Better sleep if you can."

"They're looting down there," he said. "Killing each other. Perhaps it's something in the air…" He coughed and then started to choke. I got him upright and tried to prise the packet he held from his fingers, but he reacted angrily, with surprising strength. He pulled his hand away. "I can look after myself now, old man." There were tears in his eyes as he sank back onto the pillow. "I'm just tired. Sick and tired."

"Dempsey, you're killing yourself. Let me—"

"I hope you're right, Bastable. It's taking too bloody long, though. I wish I'd had the guts to do it properly."

I stood up, telling him that I would call back later to see how he was. He closed his eyes and seemed to fall asleep.

I experienced that feeling of impotence common to many who have themselves experienced the relief of drug addiction. I knew only too well that there was little I could do for the poor, tormented wretch. He could only help himself. And Dempsey seemed genuinely haunted, perhaps by a special insight into things as they really were, perhaps by something in himself, some aspect of his own character which he could not reconcile with his moral outlook. For it was becoming increasingly clear that Dempsey, in spite of his denials, had a very moral outlook and that he didn't think much of himself.

I went to my own room along the passage and took off my jacket and trousers. I lay down on the bed in the darkness, listening to the insects hurling themselves against the woven wire of the window screens. Moonlight flooded the room. Soon I fell into a light sleep.

I woke up suddenly.

My door was creaking as it slowly opened and I looked around for a weapon, thinking that the coolies had attacked the hotel while I slept.

Then, with a sigh of relief, I saw that it was Dempsey. He was leaning almost nonchalantly on the door handle. His face was as pale as ever but he seemed to have recovered his strength.

"Sorry to disturb you, Bastable."

"Do you need help?" I got up and pulled on my trousers.

"Perhaps I do. There isn't a lot of time now." He smiled. "Not 'practical' help, though." His eyes were glazed and dreamy and I realized that he had taken some kind of stimulant to offset the effects of the opium. I hated to think what was happening both to his mind and his body. He sat down heavily on my bed.

"I'm fine." He spoke as if to reassure himself. "I just thought I'd drop in for a chat. You wanted a chat, eh? Earlier."

I sat down in the wicker armchair beside the bed. "Why not?" I said as cheerfully as I could.

"I told you there's no need to patronize me. I've come to make a sort of confession. I don't know why it should be you, Bastable. Possibly it's just because, well, you're one of the victims. Singapore, and everything…"

"It's over," I said. "And it certainly couldn't have been anything to do with you. 'The war is ceaseless. The most we can hope for are occasional moments of tranquility in the midst of the conflict.' I quote Lobkowitz."

His drugged eyes shone for a second with an ironic light. "You read him, too. I didn't think you were another Red, Bastable."

"I'm not. Neither, for that matter, is Lobkowitz."

"It's a matter of opinion."

"Besides, I speak from a great deal of experience."

"As a soldier?"

"I have been a soldier. But I have come to the conclusion that the human race is constantly in a state of tension, that those tensions make us what we are and that they will often lead to wars. The greater our ingenuity at inventing weapons, the worse the wars become."

"Oh, indeed, I agree with that last statement." He sighed. "But don't you believe it's possible for people to acknowledge the tensions and yet make harmony from those tensions, just as music is made?"

"My experience would have it otherwise. My hope, of course, is another thing. But I see little point in such a debate when the world is currently in such an appalling state. This frightful Armageddon will probably not be over until the last aerial man-o'-war falls from the skies."

"You really see it as Armageddon?"

I could not tell him what I knew: that I had already passed through three alternative versions of our world and in each seen the most hideous destruction of civilization; that I myself felt responsibility for at least one of those great wars. I merely shrugged. "Perhaps not. Perhaps there will be peace. The Russians and the Japanese have always been at loggerheads. What I can't understand is how Britain failed to stop it and why the Japs turned on us with such ferocity."

"I know why," he said.

I patted his arm. "Do you know? Or is it the opium telling you? I've been fond of opium in my time, Dempsey. My appearance was once not too different from yours. Can you believe that?"

"I thought there was something. But why—?"

"I took part in a crime," I said. "A very wicked crime. And then…" I paused. "Then I became lost."

"But you're not lost now?"

"I'm lost now, but I've decided to make the best of things. I've become a good airshipman. I love airships. There is nothing like being at the helm of one."

"I know," he said. "Of course I know. But I'll never go aloft again."

"Something happened? An accident?"

A small, wretched laugh came out of his throat. "You could call it that." He fumbled in his pocket and took something out, placing it on the bed beside him. It was a syringe. "This stuff makes you want to talk, unlike the opium." From his other pocket he took a handful of ampoules and placed them neatly beside the syringe.

I got up. "I can't let you—"

His eyes were full of pain. "Can't you?" The words had intense significance. They silenced me. I sat down again with a shrug.

He put his hand over the syringe and the ampoules and stared at me grimly. "You've no choice. I've no choice. Our choices are all gone, Bastable. For my own part, one way or another, I'm going to kill myself. You can take that for granted. And I'd rather you let me do it this way."

"I know the state of mind you're in, old man. I was in it once. And, without wishing to make a stupid comparison, I feel I've had as much reason as anyone on Earth to want to do it. But you see me alive. I've gone beyond suicide."

"Well, I haven't." Yet he hesitated. "I wanted to talk to you, Bastable."

"Then talk."

"I can't without this stuff."

Once again, I shrugged. But I knew what it was to have an unbearable weight on one's conscience. "Take a little, then," I suggested. "Just a little. And talk. But don't try to kill yourself, at least until you have confided in me."

He shuddered. "Confided! What a word. You sound like a priest."

"Just a fellow-sufferer."

"You're a bit of a prig, Bastable."

I smiled. "So I've been told by others."

"Yet you're a decent sort. And you don't judge people much. Only yourself. Am I right?"

"I'm afraid you probably are."

"You don't hold with socialism, do you? With my brand, at any rate."

"What's your brand?"

"Well, Kropotkin called it anarchism. But the word's come to mean something very different in the public mind."

"You don't blow things up, then?"

Again he began to shake. He tried to speak, but no words came. I had, accidentally, struck a nerve. I moved towards him. "I'm sorry, old man. I didn't mean…"

He drew away from me. "Get out," he said. "For God's sake leave me alone."

I felt very foolish. "Dempsey. Believe me. I meant nothing serious. I was being facetious."

"Get out!" It was almost a shout, a plea. "Get out, Bastable! The ship's coming. Save yourself, if you can."

"I'm not going to let you kill yourself." I grabbed up some of the ampoules. "I want to listen, Dempsey."

He fell back on the bed. His head hit the wall. He groaned. His body fell sideways. He had passed out.

I checked his pulse and his breathing, then I went to look for help. I recalled that there was a missionary doctor now in the hotel.

As I reached the ground floor and headed to the bar where I would find Olmeijer, I heard people near the windows begin to mutter, then to talk excitedly. The darkness outside was suddenly broken by a beam of bright light.

Olmeijer saw it. He seemed disappointed. When I reached him he muttered: "It's the ship. It's coming in." He was going to lose all his customers.

I told him to send someone to look after Dempsey, and then I ran from the hotel towards the park. My intention was to guide the ship to her mast.

To my astonishment there were already uniformed men on the ground. I rushed towards one. They must have parachuted from the ship.

"Thank God you've come," I said.

The nearest figure turned. I looked into the expressionless face of a captain in the Imperial Japanese Army. "Go back inside," he said. "Tell them that if anyone attempts to leave the building it will be bombed to rubble."

CHAPTER TEN

Lost Hopes

We were never to discover how the Japanese had found us. Either they had traced the wireless messages or they had trailed and destroyed the rescue ship. The fact was there was nothing we could do against them.

Soon Olmeijer's place was full of small soldiers in off-white uniforms, their politeness to their prisoners contrasting with the long bayonets fixed on their rifles. The officer had a grim, self-controlled manner, but occasionally, it seemed to me, an expression of straightforward hatred crossed his face when he looked at us. We stood with our baggage (if we had any) in the middle of the floor. The women were sent aboard first. The Japs had managed to get the mast working and had winched the ship to ground level.

It was a large, modern ship. I was surprised that they had felt they could spare it, merely to pick up a few civilians, but I guessed that it had already been patrolling the area when its captain had been alerted to our presence.

Nye was closer to the windows than I. He turned to me. "My

God, they've fired the town!" He pointed, addressing the officer. "You damned barbarians! Why did you have to do that?"

"Barbarians?" The Japanese captain smiled sardonically. "I am amused you should think that of us, Englishman, after what you did to us."

"We did nothing! Whatever happened was a mistake. It suits you to blame us."

The captain dismissed this. "However, we have not set fire to the buildings. It's your own workers. A riot of some kind. I gather they're on their way, *en masse*."

It was credible. Thinking that they might get free of the island aboard a ship, the coolies could have persuaded themselves that it was possible to capture the vessel and sail it to freedom.

"Don't worry," continued the Jap, "we intend to protect you as well as ourselves." His voice, pleasant and yet sharp, had a degree of contempt in it. I saw that Nye was upset by the exchange.

Nye blustered a little, but he could not argue with the man's logic. We had far more to fear from the coolies, immediately at any rate, than from the Japanese.

It was possible to smell the smoke from where we stood; and traces of red firelight were reflected in the windows and mirrors of Olmeijer's. The Dutchman had given up his despair and was now offering to serve drinks to his new customers (as he saw them). I think he had half a hope that Rowe Island was to be occupied and that he would be allowed to continue (as a neutral) to run the hotel. The soldiers motioned him to join us at the centre of the floor. He sat down on one of his own tables. I thought he might be going to cry. "I am Dutch," he told the officer. "I am a private hotelier. A civilian. You cannot just remove me from the place I have spent most of my life building."

"We have orders to arrest all Europeans," said the Japanese. "And you are most definitely European, sir. We have nothing against the Dutch. However, if you were to be realistic you would understand that your country is an ally of Britain and that it is only a matter of days before you are involved in this war."

"But we are not involved today!"

"Not as far as I know. Essentially our mission is to evacuate you from the island."

"And what will happen to us?" asked Nye, still in an aggressive mood.

"You will be interned for the duration of hostilities."

"We're not spies!"

"Neither were those you interned in your South African war, you'll recall."

"That was entirely different. The reasons were complex…"

"Our reasons are also complex. You are foreign belligerents, potentially dangerous to our War Effort."

"My God! And you infer that *we* are hypocritical!"

"You will not deny, sir, that this is effectively a military base."

"It's a mining concern!"

"But very useful as a fueling station. We shall be leaving troops behind. A garrison. This is conquered territory. When you go outside you will see that the Japanese flag now flies over the airfield."

"Then why remove us? Is it usual practice?"

"It has become so. You will be interned at the European civilian prisoner-of-war camp on Rishiri."

"Where the hell is Rishiri?"

"It's a small island off the coast of Hokkaido," said one of the Irish priests. Hokkaido was the large island north of Honshu, Japan's main island. "Quite a pretty place, as I recollect. We did some missionary work there a few years ago."

The Japanese captain smiled. "You'll have to concentrate on Europeans now, Father. But you will have plenty of time to make converts, I'm sure."

Nye fell silent. He finished the last of his gin fizz with the air of a man who was not likely to see another again for many years.

With the women gone, the older men were next to be taken from the room. The Japanese were by no means cruel to us. Those who were too weak to move easily were helped by soldiers, who even carried bundles and suitcases for their prisoners, shouldering their rifles in order to do so. There was no point in trying to resist them, and they knew it. The ship's guns could have destroyed Olmeijer's in seconds, and we had so many other people to consider.

A few minutes later the Japanese captain went outside and then returned to issue commands to his men. The rifles were unshouldered and they ran into the night, leaving only one man to guard us. We heard shouts, then shots; a terrible scream which rose and fell, then rose again: the scream of a mob.

"The coolies!" Olmeijer waddled towards the window. We all followed him. The guard did not attempt to stop us. He stood by the door, looking back in some trepidation.

The red firelight silhouetted the Malays and Chinese now trying to rush the airship which was defended by a line of well-disciplined Japanese soldiers. The coolies were badly armed, though one or two had rifles and pistols. For the most part the best weapons they had been able to muster were parangs and large picks and hammers. Panic, anger and hatred drove them against the rifle-fire. Not a bullet was wasted. They continued to fall until the corpses of the dead and wounded hampered the advance of those who still lived.

They appeared to have some sort of rough organization, however, because they now fell back. Their efforts were being directed by a figure in a crumpled European suit armed with a pistol.

I recognized him as he disappeared with the surviving coolies into the darkness.

How Dempsey had managed to leave the hotel in the

condition in which I'd last seen him I didn't know. But there he was, capering like a maniac, helping the coolies in their desperate attack.

They came in from two sides now, trying to divide the Japanese fire. This time two or three soldiers were hit. They retreated in order until they were closer to the ship.

Nye whispered to me: "This would be our chance to get out of here. Rush the guard and get into the bush, eh?"

I considered this. "Between the Japanese and the surviving coolies we'd have no chance," I said. "There isn't any food to speak of, either."

"You've no guts, Bastable."

"Perhaps. But I've a great deal of experience," I told him. "There's quite likely to be an exchange of civilian prisoners of war. We could all be in England in a matter of weeks."

"But what if we're not?"

"My view is that we'll be better off with the Japs for the moment. If we're going to escape, let's escape from somewhere closer to Russian territory."

Nye was disgusted. "You're not exactly impetuous, are you, Bastable?"

"I suppose not." I had seen too much of warfare and destruction in three worlds to place much value on romantic, impulsive schemes. I preferred to bide my time. I let Nye think what he liked and noticed that, without my agreement, he made no attempt to get free of Olmeijer's.

The firing outside continued but was more spasmodic. Below, in the town, the flames were rising higher. Firelight was reflected on the white hull of the Japanese ship as it swayed slowly at its mast.

Dempsey must have made full use of his stimulants. From time to time I saw him, sometimes with a pistol, sometimes with a parang, leaping here and there amongst the shrubs and trees surrounding the airpark. He was demented. For what obscure, perhaps sentimental, reasons he had leagued himself with the coolies, I could not fathom. Perhaps he saw hope in turning them against the Japanese and saving the Europeans, but I doubted it. In his ragged jacket and trousers he was distinguished from the rabble largely by the fact that he was evidently in control. He had been trained in the navy and his old instincts for leadership were coming out.

The Japanese had also identified him and their fire was concentrated against him. He was courting their bullets. To me, it seemed he wanted them to kill him. He had been talking of suicide and perhaps this was in his eyes a more positive way of dying. Nonetheless he showed courage and I could only admire the way he harried the Japs, sending in coolies from every direction, sometimes at once, sometimes from a single angle.

His eyes glittered, filled with flames. There was a strange, cold grin on his lips. And for a moment I was consumed by an enormous sense of comradeship for him. It was as if I looked at some other incarnation of myself, in those dreadful days before I had learned to live with the guilt, the pain and the hopelessness of my own situation.

Then Dempsey rushed for the ship, all the remaining coolies at his back. He hacked down two soldiers before they could defend themselves. He fenced with the parang, warding off bayonets and bullets. He took another two of the Japanese and had actually reached the gangway into the gondola when, both arms lifted as if to some blood-greedy battle-god, he dropped.

I saw his body lying spreadeagled on the gangway. It twitched for a moment or two. I didn't know if a bullet had struck him or if the stimulants had caused a stroke. The captain, sword in hand, ran up to the body and turned it over, instructing two of his men to drag it inside.

I heard one of the soldiers utter his name: "Dempsey". And I wondered how on earth they could know him.

With Dempsey down, the coolies were quickly scattered. The captain returned to Olmeijer's and ordered the rest of us aboard the ship. I asked him: "How's the white man? Is he shot? Did he collapse?" But the captain refused to answer.

Nye said: "Look here, captain. You could tell us if Dempsey's alive or dead!"

The Japanese drew in his breath and looked hard at Nye. "You have certain rights as a civilian prisoner of war. Captain Dempsey also has certain rights. However, I am not obliged to answer enquiries as to the fate of another prisoner."

"You inhuman devil. It's not a question of rights, but simple decency!"

The Japanese captain gestured with his sword and gave a command in his own tongue. The guards began to march us out.

As we left, I heard him say: "If we were not a civilized people none of you would be alive now. And Captain Dempsey would have been torn to pieces by my men."

The captain seemed mad. Perhaps he did not enjoy his trade. Many soldiers did not, when real warfare developed.

I wondered what crime Dempsey had committed to make him so loathed by those who believed him guilty of it. It was almost certain, anyway, that he had paid the price of the crime with his life. I regretted very much that he had not had time to tell me his own story.

An hour later we were aloft, leaving the remnants of Rowe Island and its population behind. Through a small porthole I could see the flames spreading through the town. They had even caught some of the foliage. Small figures ran about in the inferno. It was still possible to hear shots as the Japanese continued to defend their newly conquered territory.

Our quarters were crowded, but not intolerable. Dempsey was not amongst us. Everyone assumed he had been killed.

It was dawn by the time we had gained our cruising altitude. Most of us were silent, dozing to the steady drumming of the engines. I suppose we were all wondering what would become of us once we reached the civilian camp on Rishiri. If the war continued as I had known other wars to continue, then it might be years before we were free.

I realized, with no particular dismay, that I might even die of old age before this particular conflict were resolved.

I was almost relieved that in no way was my fate any longer in my own hands.

BOOK TWO

"NEITHER MASTER NOR SLAVE!"

CHAPTER ONE

The Camp on Rishiri

The civilian prisoner-of-war camp was well organized and clean. The food was simple and adequate and our treatment was by no means harsh. There was a permanent Red Cross supervisor and a representative of the Swiss Government who had elected at the invitation of the Japanese to act as a sort of umpire. There were civilians of most nationalities here and those belonging to neutral countries (no longer the Dutch) were efficiently repatriated, so long as they could prove their identity and place of origin. There were a good many angry Poles, Bohemians and Latvians present, for instance. Technically they were Russian citizens, but vociferously denied their loyalty to any land save their own. Since Poles and Slovaks were fighting in Russian armies there was not a great deal of weight to their protestations.

I found the mixture of races fascinating and made the most of my imprisonment to learn as much as I could about the world in which I had found myself. Here was a future in which O'Bean had not existed, yet it contained many of the inventions familiar to me in that future where I had originally encountered General O. T.

Shaw. It seemed that whether they were the work of an individual genius or a variety of hard-working scientists, the airships and the sub-aquatic boats, the electrical wonders, the wireless telegraph and so on, would nonetheless come into existence at some time. In this world Britain's Empire was even larger than in my own. Certain mainland territories in South and Central America were hers, as were some parts of what I had known as the Southern United States. These had been regained, it appeared, during the American Civil War, when Britain had lent positive support to the Confederacy in return for control over coastal regions. With the victory of the Confederacy it had suited everyone, I learned, to retain this contact. The lands had been leased from the CSA for a period of a hundred years. This meant that in thirty years' time, the Confederacy would reclaim them. I was curious as to whether slavery continued to flourish and learned to my surprise that not only did it not, but that economically it had suited everyone to see a strong black middle class emerging. In America there was greater racial equality than in my own day! North and South were virtually autonomous and these smaller units seemed to have produced greater coherence rather than less. Although America was not quite so rich in industry, not quite so powerful a military nation, she seemed in many other ways to have benefited from the truce which had followed the Civil War and allowed both sides to recover and begin to trade.

France, on the other hand, was no longer a Great Power. She had never recovered from the Franco-Prussian Wars. Germany now controlled much of the old French Empire and the French themselves seemed content enough in the main, without the responsibilities of their colonies. Germany had become a close ally of Britain, although not bound to join in the current conflict. She formed part of an alliance with the Scandinavian countries, a very powerful trading pact which suited everyone. Austria-Hungary mouldered on, a romantic, decaying Empire, constantly in debt, constantly being helped out by richer nations. The only new Great Power of any significance was the Ottoman Empire, which had expanded significantly into Africa and the Middle East to form a strong Islamic union. Greece, I learned, was all but non-existent. Most of her people were now Moslems and to all intents and purposes Turkish. The Japanese Empire controlled large areas of what had been China and her inroads along borders of the Russian Empire had been the chief reason for the present struggle. I learned why the Japanese attacked British targets with far greater ferocity than they attacked others. They believed that Britain had deliberately started the war, with a raid on Hiroshima. I was reminded of my own part—my own guilt—in a similar raid, when I had sailed aboard the flagship of General Shaw.

If I had known only one world I might have thought that History was repeating itself, but I knew that it was human nature which lay at the root of History and that no matter where I found myself I was bound to discover superficial similarities expressing and exemplifying that nature. It was human idealism and human impatience and human despair which continued to produce these terrible wars. Human virtues and vices, mixed and confused in individuals, created what we called "History". Yet I could see no way in which the vicious circle of aspiration and desperation might ever be broken. We were all victims of our own imagination. This I had realized in all my strange journeyings across what Mrs. Persson calls "the multiverse". The very thing which makes us human, which produces the best, is also the thing which will make us behave worse than the maddest wild beast could ever behave. We live through example and emulation which can turn into envy if circumstances create for us misfortunes. That is all I have come to believe, and I am not entirely sure I believe that. But I am reconciled to human nature, if not to human folly, and that is what my own particular misfortunes have achieved for me.

Olmeijer was soon in his element once again. He somehow

managed to get himself put in charge of the camp shop and ran it
with all the grandeur of a Chef de la Maison at the Ritz.

Nye joined a group of English and Australian merchant
seamen who had been captured at the fall of Shanghai. They spent
most of their time choosing sides for rugby football games and
talking about home. I supposed that this was how they managed
to avoid thinking too much about the truth of their situation, but I
could only stand half-an-hour or so of their schoolboy stuff. I knew
very well that not long before my first visit to Teku Benga I might
well have joined in with some enthusiasm. I had changed beyond
redemption. I would never be quite the same as the idealistic
and naïve young army officer who had first led his men into the
mountains in search of the bandit, Sharan Kang. I felt, indeed,
like a cross between Rip Van Winkle and the Flying Dutchman,
with a touch of the Wandering Jew besides. I sometimes felt that
I had lived for as long as the human race had existed.

Quite soon after arriving at the camp I myself fell in with a
mixed bag of civilian airshipmen, the survivors of a variety of
wrecks. Some had been accidentally shot down, others had been
rescued by Japanese patrols. Some had simply been lost in the
general chaos and wandered into Japanese hands. I learned that
all merchant airships now moved in convoys these days, protected
by military vessels.

It was about a week later that "Peewee" Wilson attached
himself to me. He was a thin-faced, bulbous man, with an
awkward, unspontaneous way of moving, a flat forehead and
cheekbones and a reddish discoloration under the eyes of the sort
I often identify with a certain mental imbalance. He approached
me as I came out of Olmeijer's hut. He regarded me, he said, as a
fellow intellectual, someone who had "a bit more education than
most of these riff-raff". Since there were a number of clergymen
and academics amongst the prisoners in our compound alone,
as well as a couple of journalists, I did not find his remarks

particularly flattering. He wore a khaki shirt and a striped tie, grey flannel trousers and, no matter what the temperature, would often have on a tweed sports-jacket with leather patches on the elbows. He was a bore. He was, in fact, the camp bore. Every army unit has one, every airship crew has one, every office and factory in the world doubtless has one. However, Wilson was, I'll admit, a bit above the average bore.

He drew me across the compound to the wire fence corner. Leaning against one of the struts of the fence was a short, moody Slav in a dirty peasant shirt. I had seen him before. His name was Makhno and he was from the Ukraine. For bizarre idealistic reasons of his own he had elected to make his way to Tokyo in the cause of international brotherhood. He was an anarchist, I gathered, of the old Kropotkin school and, I thought then, like most anarchists would rather talk than anything else. He was a likable enough fellow who, having failed to convert the camp, kept his own counsel. Wilson introduced us. "This chap's not too good with the English," he said. "I talk a spot of Rooshian, but I'm having trouble getting through to him. We were talking about money."

"You're trying to buy something?" I asked.

"No, no. *Money*. International finance and that."

"Aha." I exchanged glances with the Ukrainian, who raised a sardonic eyebrow.

"Now I'm a socialist, right?" continued Wilson. "Have been all my life. You might ask what we mean by the word socialism, and you'd be correct in doing so, because socialism can mean many different things to many different people…" He went on in this vein, doubtless word for word repeating himself for the nth time. There are some people who never appear to realize to what degree they have this habit. I have come to believe that it has the effect on them of a soothing lullaby sung to themselves. It has a completely opposite effect, of course, on anyone attempting (or forced) to listen to them.

The anarchist, Makhno, was not bothering to listen. It was obvious that he could understand many of the words but that he had instinctively recognized Wilson's type.

"Now *this* chap," Wilson stabbed an unhealthy finger in Makhno's direction, "would call himself a socialist. I suppose the term would be 'anarcho-socialist'. That is to say, he believes in the brotherhood of man, the emancipation of the working classes of the world and so on and so forth. He comes, after all, from a so-called socialist country, though what it's doing with an emperor still there, for all he's got no real power, I don't know. And he's against his own government."

"The Russian government," said Makhno. "I am against all governments. Including the so-called Ukrainian Rada, which is only a puppet of the Central Government in Petersburg."

"Just so," said Wilson, dismissing this. "So you're a socialist and you're against socialists. Am I right or wrong?"

"Kerensky's Duma is socialist in name only," said Makhno in gloomy, Slavic tones. "In name only."

"Exactly my own point. Not proper socialists. Just Tories under another name, right?"

"Politicians," said Makhno laconically.

"That's where you're wrong, old chap. Just because they're not real socialists doesn't mean that real socialists can't make good politicians."

I was already trying to extricate myself from this, but Wilson held onto my arm. "Hang on a minute, old man. I want you to umpire this one. Now, what do we mean by this word 'politics' of ours? See, I'm an engineer by profession, and I like to think a pretty good one. To me politics is just a matter of getting the engineering right. If you have a machine which functions properly without much attention, then it's obviously a good machine. That's what politics should be about. And if the machine has simple working parts which any layman can understand, then it's, as it were, your democratic machine. Am I right or am I wrong?"

"Crazy," said Makhno, and scratched his nose.

"What?"

"You're not right or wrong. You're crazy."

I was amused by this and Makhno could tell, but Wilson was baffled.

"Sane, I'd say," he said. "Very sane indeed. Like a good machine. That's sane, isn't it? What's more sane than a properly functioning steam turbine, for instance?"

"Rationalist nonsense," pronounced Makhno, and rolled the "r" in that ironic way only Slavs have.

"And what about your own romantic twaddle?" Wilson wanted to know. "Blow everything up and start again, eh?"

"No worse a solution than yours. But this is not what I argued."

"It's what it comes down to, old chap. That's your anarchism for you. Boom!" And he laughed as one who had never known humour.

Although I felt sorry for Makhno (while having little sympathy with his politics) I had had quite enough of this. With a murmur of vague apology I began to move away, to where some of my acquaintances were standing, smoking their pipes and talking airship talk, which at that moment was preferable to anything Wilson had to offer.

Wilson stopped me. "Hang on just a sec, old man. What I want you to tell me is this: without government, who makes the decisions?"

"The individual," said Makhno.

I shrugged. "Given the hypothesis as it's put," I said, "our Ukrainian friend is absolutely right. Who else could make a decision?"

"Just for himself?"

"By consensus," said Makhno.

"Ha!" Wilson was triumphant. "Ha! And what's that but democratic socialism. Which is exactly what I believe in."

"I thought you believed in machines." I couldn't resist this jab.

Wilson missed my small irony as he had missed all Makhno's. "A democratic—socialist—machine," he said, as if to a child.

"That is not anarchism," said Makhno stubbornly. But he was not trying to convince Wilson. If anything, he was trying to drive him away.

"I can see some of my pals want a word," I said to Wilson. I winked at Makhno and made off. But Wilson pursued me. "You're an airshipman by all accounts, as are these fellows. Don't you believe in using the best machinery, the engines least likely to let you down, the control systems which will work as simply as possible…?"

"Airships aren't countries," I said. Unfortunately an unsuspecting second officer from the destroyed *Duchess of Salford* heard me without noticing Wilson.

"They can be," he said. "Like small countries. I mean, everyone has to learn to get on together…"

I left him to Wilson. When he realized what he had let himself in for a look of patent dismay crossed his young face. I waved at him behind Wilson's back and sauntered off.

It was to be one of my easier escapes from the Bore of Rishiri. The fact that I was a prisoner and beginning, like many others, to fret a great deal was bad enough. It was Purgatory. But "Peewee" was making it Hell. I am still surprised that nobody murdered him. He became impossible to avoid.

At first we tried joshing him to get rid of him and then laughing at him, then downright rudeness, but it was useless to try to insult him or alter him in his course. We would sometimes offend him, but he would either laugh it off or, if hurt, return in a few minutes. And I had everyone's sympathy because he continued, no matter what I said or did, to claim me as his closest friend.

I think that must be why, when Nye approached me with his half-baked escape plan, I agreed to join in against all common sense. He and his fellow rugger enthusiasts meant to go under the wire at night and try to capture one of the two Japanese motor-torpedo-boats which had recently anchored in Rishiri's tiny harbour. From there Nye and Co. intended to try for the Russian mainland which had not fallen to the Japs.

There had been a number of attempted escapes, of course, but all of them had been unsuccessful. Our guards were vigilant; there were two small scouting airships keeping the tiny island under surveillance. There were searchlights, dogs, the whole paraphernalia of a prison. Moreover, the island was used as a fueling station for raids against Russia (which is why we were there—to stop the base from being bombed) so it usually had several large airships at mast near the harbour.

It was true, as Nye argued, that no military aerial vessels were in evidence at that moment, but I was not sure that, as he put it, this was "the best chance of getting clear we'll ever have".

I did believe that there was a small chance of escape as well as a fair chance of being killed or wounded. But I argued to myself that even if I were wounded I should spend time in the hospital away from Wilson.

"Very well, Nye," I said. "You can count me in."

"Good man." He patted my shoulder.

That night we assembled in twos and threes at Olmeijer's shop. The Dutchman was not in evidence. He would have been too portly to have squeezed himself into the tunnel Nye and his rugger chums had been digging. It was usual to meet in the hut in the evening, to play table tennis or the variety of board games supplied by the Red Cross. We had only occasional trouble from the guards, who were inclined to look in on us at random. Because they did not check our numbers, we stood a fair chance of all getting down the tunnel before they suspected anything. A few of the airshipmen had elected to stay behind to cover us.

Nye was to go first and I was to go last. One by one the men disappeared into the earth. And it was as I was about to follow them that I realized Fate was almost certainly singling me out for unusual punishment. Wilson walked though the door of the hut.

I was halfway down. I think I remember smiling at him weakly.

"My lord, old man! What are you up to?" He asked. Then he brightened. "An escape, eh? Good show. A secret, is it? Shan't breathe a word. I take it anyone can join in."

"Um," I said. "Actually Nye…"

"My pal Nye, eh? His idea. Jolly good. That's all right with me, old man. I trust Nye implicitly. And he'd want me along."

One of the airshipmen near the window hissed that a couple of guards were on their way.

I ducked into the tunnel and began to wriggle along it. There was no time to argue with Wilson. I heard his voice behind me.

"Make way for a little 'un."

I knew that he had joined me in the tunnel before the light vanished as the airshipmen above replaced the floor boards.

I seemed to crawl for eternity, with Wilson muttering and apologizing, constantly bumping into my feet, criticizing what he called the "poor engineering job" of the tunnel. He wondered why they hadn't thought of asking him for his expert help.

We emerged into sweet-smelling darkness. Behind us was the wire and the lights of the camp. We were close to the earth road which wound down to the harbour. Nye and the merchant seamen were whispering and gesticulating in the darkness, just as if they were still choosing sides for a game.

Wilson said in a voice which seemed unnaturally loud, even for him: "What's the problem? Need a volunteer?"

Nye came up to me urgently. "Good God, man. Why did you tell him?"

"I didn't. He found out just as the guards were on their way."

"I thought you could do with an extra chap," said Wilson. "So I volunteered. Don't forget I'm an expert engineer."

I heard someone curse and murmur: "Shoot the blighter." Peewee, of course, was oblivious.

Nye sighed. "We'd better start getting down to the harbour. If we're separated—"

He was interrupted by the unmistakable growl of airship engines high overhead. "Damn! That complicates things."

The sound of the engines grew louder and louder and it was evident that the ships were coming in lower. We began to duck and weave through the shrubs and trees at the side of the road, heading for the harbour.

Then, suddenly, there was light behind us, and gunfire, the steady pounding of artillery. A dying scream as a bomb descended some distance from the camp. Up the road came several trucks full of soldiers, as well as a couple of armoured cars and some motor-bicycles. The firing continued until I realized that the ships were attacking. Something whizzed past me, just above my head. It felt like a one-man glider. These ingenious devices were far more manageable than parachutes in landing troops. It seemed there was a raid on and we had become caught in the middle of it.

Nye and his lads decided not to vary from their plan. "We'll use the confusion," he said.

Wilson called: "I say, steady on. Perhaps we should wait and see what—"

"No time!" shouted Nye. "We don't know what this is all about. Let's get to that boat."

"But suppose—"

"Shut up, Wilson," I said. I was prepared to follow Nye's lead. I felt I had little choice now.

"Wait!" cried the engineer. "Let's just stop and think for a minute. If we keep our heads—"

"You're about to lose yours to a samurai sword," called Nye. "Now for God's sake shut up, Wilson. Either stay where you are or come with us quietly."

"Quietly? I wonder what you mean to say when you say—"

His droning voice was a greater source of fear than any bombs or bullets. We all put on an excellent burst of speed. By now machine-guns were going, both from the ground and from the rear. I have never prayed before for another human being's death, but I prayed that night that somebody would take Wilson directly between the eyes and save us.

The Japanese were all making for the camp. As a result we were lucky. They weren't looking for escaped prisoners just yet. Even when we were spotted, we were taken for enemy soldiers. We were shot at, but we were not pursued.

We reached the outskirts of the town. Getting through the streets unobserved was going to be the difficult part.

Again we were lucky in that whatever was going on behind us was diverting all troops, all attention. It was Wilson crying: "I say, you fellows, wait for me!" that brought us the greatest danger. A small detachment of Japanese infantry heard his voice and immediately began to fire along the alley we had entered. Nye went down, together with a couple of others.

I kneeled beside Nye. I tested his pulse. He had been shot in the back of the head and was quite dead. Another chap was dead, also, but the survivor was only slightly wounded. He got his arm over my shoulder and we continued to make for the harbour. By this time we were fairly hysterical and were yelling wildly at Wilson as Japanese soldiers opened fire again behind us. "Shut up, you damned fool! Nye is dead!"

"Dead? He should have been more careful…"

"Shut up, Wilson!"

We got to the quayside and went straight into the water, as planned, swimming for the nearest boat, a white-and-red blur in the misty electric light from the harbour. I heard Wilson behind me.

"I say, you chaps. I say! Didn't you realize I couldn't swim?"

This intelligence seemed to lend me greater energy. Supporting the wounded man, I swam slowly towards the MTB. Some of the seamen were already climbing its sides. I was relieved to hear no further gun shots. Perhaps we had managed to surprise them, after all.

By the time I eventually got to the MTB a rope ladder had been thrown down for me. I lifted the wounded man on to it, holding it while he ascended. I think I could still hear Wilson's dreadful cries from the harbour:

"I say, chaps. Hang on a minute. Can somebody send a boat to fetch me?"

I hardened my heart. At that moment I must admit I didn't give a fig for Wilson's life.

By the time I reached the deck I was gasping with exhaustion. I looked around me, expecting to see captured Japanese sailors. Instead I saw the white uniforms of Russian Navy personnel. A young lieutenant, his cap on the side of his head, his tunic unbuttoned, a revolver and a sabre in his hands, saluted me with his sword. "Welcome aboard, sir," he said in perfect English. He grinned at me with that wild, careless grin which only Russians have. "We both appear to have had the same idea," he said. "I am Lieutenant Mitrofanovitch, at your service. We took this boat only twenty minutes before you arrived."

"And the airships back there?"

"Russian. We are rescuing the prisoners, I hope, at this very moment."

"You're using an awful lot of stuff for a few prisoners," I said.

"While the prisoners are on the island," said Mitrofanovitch pragmatically, "we cannot bomb the fueling station."

One of the English seamen said. "Poor bloody Nye. He died for absolutely nothing."

I leaned on the rail. From the quayside I could still hear Wilson's awful voice, pleading and desperate: the wailing of a frightened child.

CHAPTER TWO

Back in Service

If someone had told me, before I ever entered the Temple of Teku Benga, that I should one day be glad to join the Russian Service, I should not only have laughed at them I should, if they had persisted, probably have punched them on the nose. In those days Russia was the greatest menace to our frontiers in India. There was often the threat of open war, for it was well-known that they had territorial ambitions in Afghanistan, if nowhere else. The fact that the Japanese Empire and the Russian Empire had clashed over which parts of South-East Asia and China came under their control was probably fortunate for the British. The war might well have taken a different turn, with Japan and Britain as allies, if Russian ambitions had not, in this world, been diverted towards the crumbling remains of the Chinese Empire. A great deal of the reason for this, of course, was Kerensky himself. The old President of Russia (and the chief power in the so-called Union of Independent Slavic Republics—fundamentally the countries conquered by Imperial Russia before the socialist Revolution) was anxious to keep the friendship of Europe and America and this meant that he had become extremely cautious about offending us. Russia needed to import a great many manufactured goods even now, and she needed markets for her agricultural produce. Moreover, she required as much foreign investment as she could get and was especially interested in attracting British and American capital. She had taken huge steps forward since the successful— and almost bloodless—Revolution of 1905 which had occurred at a time when another war between Russia and Japan was brewing. Her brand of humanist socialism had produced almost universal literacy and her medical facilities were amongst the best in the world. She had produced a thriving and liberal middle class and it was very rare, these days, to encounter the kind of poverty for which Russia, when I was a boy, was famous. All in all, even amongst the most conservative people, there was no doubt that Russia and her dominions were much improved by Kerensky and his socialists.

Whatever the historical reasons, there was nothing dishonourable in joining the Russians against our common enemy. When we were taken, by sub-aquatic liner, first to Vladivostok and then, by airship, to Khabarovsk, I wondered how long it would be before I could begin doing something again. The imprisonment alone had left me frustrated. When news came through that any British citizens with airship experience were needed for the aerial arm of the Russian Volunteer Fleet and that Whitehall was actively encouraging us to join up, I put my name down immediately, as did most of the chaps I was with. Those few of us, like myself, with military experience were given the choice of serving on armed merchantmen, flying in convoys, or on the escorting aerial frigates and cruisers themselves. I elected to join the frigates. I had no particular urge to kill my fellow men but wanted to take something less than a passive role through the rest of this particular war. I have learned from my experiences that hatred and racial antagonism can be manufactured by the politicians of any one country against any other, so I was no longer the patriot I had been. Personally, however, and I know now that this was an infantile impulse, I felt that I had been put to a great deal of trouble by the Japanese and I might as well fight them as anyone else. I also, I must admit, rather hoped there would not be too much conflict. I wanted to fly good, fast ships. And here, at last, was my chance.

We had a two-week training programme in and around Samara, in which we learned the specifics of the Russian ships, which were mainly built and equipped according to the designs of the great engineer Pyatnitski and at that time were amongst the most modern in the world; then we were assigned to various ships to get general experience. I joined the aerial cruiser *Vassarion Belinsky*. She was a fine, easy-handling ship, sailing out of the Lermontov Airpark a few miles to the north of Odessa, that marvelous cosmopolitan seaport from which have come so many fine Russian-speaking poets, novelists, painters and intellectuals. I had a few days' leave in Odessa before we sailed and I enjoyed those days to the full. Being on the Black Sea the port was relatively untouched by the war and there was more merchant shipping in her harbours than there was naval. Her streets were crowded with people of every colour and nation. She smelled of spices, of the food of five continents, and there was a merry, carefree quality about her, even in wartime, which seemed to me to exemplify the very best of the Slavic soul.

Odessa has a large Jewish population (for it is, of course, the capital of Russian Jewry beyond the Pale, even though the Pale itself, together with all anti-Semitic laws, has been abolished in Kerensky's Russia) and so is full of music, intelligent commercial enterprise—and Romance. I fell in love with her immediately. I know of no other city quite like her and often wish that I could have spent longer exploring her winding streets, her avenues and promenades, her resorts and watering places. She is not, strictly speaking, a Russian city. She is Ukrainian, and the Ukrainians will insist very firmly that the "goat-beards" (their word for Great Russians) are interlopers, that Kiev, capital of the Ukraine, is the true centre of Slavic culture, that the Muscovites are upstarts, parvenus, johnny-come-latelies, tyrants, imperialists, thieves, carpet-baggers and almost anything else of the kind you care to think of. It is true that the government of Moscow has most power over the Ukraine, but there is a spirit of freedom about Odessa which, I think, denies any of its denizens' allegations.

In Odessa I also learned a great deal about the progress of the war. On land the Japanese had made many early gains but were now being beaten back by Russian and British infantry—indeed, they had held less territory than before the war. They were still pretty powerful in the air and at sea, and were masters of strategy, but all in all we were optimistic about the way the conflict was turning, for the Dutch and Portuguese were also on our side and although their navies were not large they were extremely capable.

It is certain that the war would have been as good as over if it had not been for Russia's domestic problems. These tended, amongst Odessa's population, to be a more important topic than the war itself. Perhaps because of the war, there was a threat of revolution in several parts of the UISR. Indeed, whole parts of the Ukraine were currently in the hands of large armies calling themselves Free Cossacks—many of them deserters from various cavalry regiments. I gathered that they were intense Slavophils, opposed to Kerensky's "Europeanization" of their lands, who were "nationalists" in that they argued for the independence of all territories currently making up the Russian Empire—Bohemia, Moravia, Poland, Finland, Latvia, Estonia, Bulgaria and so on. Their policies and demands seemed vague, though socialistic in terminology, even when I heard them discussed from all aspects, but if it was possible to argue forever about the interpretation of their ideology, all agreed to a degree of fascination with the leading personality amongst the revolutionists, the mysterious man known popularly as the Steel Tsar. He was believed to have come originally from Georgia and his real name was thought to be Josef Vissarionovich Djugashvili, an ex-priest with a record of messianism. He was known as the Steel Tsar because he tended to wear an ancient metal helmet covering most of his face. There were many explanations of this; some thought him disfigured in battle, others thought that his features had been hideously deformed since birth. He was supposed to have a withered arm, be a hunchback, have artificial legs, and not be a human being at all, but some sort of automaton.

Because of the atmosphere surrounding Djugashvili, I myself became quite as curious about him as the natives. I followed the news of the Free Cossacks as eagerly as I followed news of the British airship battles in the skies of the Pacific.

In Odessa I met one of the chaps with whom I had been imprisoned. He was about to join a British merchantman. He told me that Wilson, too, was working for the Russians, but he wasn't sure where. "Some sort of engineering job, I gather." Olmeijer was in Yalta, managing a State-owned hotel. The worst news, however, concerned Dempsey. "I heard he jumped it before we ever got to Japan. Seemed so scared of what they'd do to him that, wounded as he was, he preferred to dive out. God knows why they hated him so. Do you have any idea, Bastable?"

I shook my head. But again I experienced that peculiar frisson, a sort of recognition.

My experience of Odessa was as intense as it was brief and I missed it, when I left for the airpark on the train, as if I had lived there for years.

The *Vassarion Belinsky* was a joy. She used liquid ballast which could, like her gas, be heated or cooled to alter her weight and her ascent acceleration was, if we needed it, rocket-like in its speed. She had a top-speed of 200 mph but could be pushed quite a bit faster than that with a good wind behind her. She could turn and dive like a porpoise and there was almost nothing you couldn't do with her. All the crew, except me, were Russian. Captain Korzeniowski was a thoroughly experienced airshipman of the old school with an excellent grasp of English. Of course the name meant a great deal to me but I barely recognized him since he was clean-shaven. He did not appear to know me at all and I was forced to remind myself that few of us come to my understanding of the nature of our existence. He knew nothing of "alternate worlds". My own Russian was, naturally, limited, but I have a facility for languages. I soon knew enough to carry on normal conversations, while much of our day-to-day jargon was English, since England had for many years maintained herself as successfully in the air as she had on the sea.

As we left Lermontov Airpark on a cool, sunny dawn, gaining height through a slow, gentle curve which revealed more and more of the steppe through our observation ports, Captain Korzeniowski broke open his orders on the control deck and, standing with his back to our helmsman, informed his officers of the *Vassarion Belinsky*'s mission.

I was not the only one both surprised and disappointed. It seemed we were victims of a typical piece of Muscovite bureaucratic muddle, and there I was (since I had signed up for a minimum of a year) with absolutely nothing I could do about it.

Korzeniowski's heavy Polish face was sober and his voice sonorous as he began to read the orders. With typical courtesy, he spoke English for my benefit.

"We are to proceed at all fastest speed to Yekaterinaslav, which is currently sustaining heavy attack from rebel forces. We are to join other ships under the command of Air Admiral Krassnov." He pinched his eyebrows together. It was obvious that he had no taste for the commission, which would involve him in giving orders which would inevitably lead to the death of other Slavs.

Everyone was agitated by the news. They had been expecting to defend their country against the Japanese. Instead, they were assigned to domestic policing duties of a kind which all the officers found distasteful and demeaning. I did not really mind missing a scrap with the Japanese, but I was bitterly sorry that I was unlikely to see any real aerial action. I had joined the Service out of a mixture of desperation and boredom. I appeared to be doomed to a continuation of those circumstances. Moreover, I should sooner or later have blood on my hands, and it would be the blood of people I had absolutely nothing against. I had no idea of the issues. Socialists are always quarreling amongst themselves, because of the strong element of messianism in their creeds, and I could see little difference between Kerensky's brand or Djugashvili's. My only consolation was that at least I might have the opportunity of observing the Steel Tsar (or at any rate his works) at first hand.

Pilniak, a second lieutenant of about my own age, with huge brown eyes and a rather girlish face (though he was in no way effeminate) grasped my uniformed shoulder (like him I wore the pale blue of the Russian Volunteer Airforce) and laughed.

"Well, Mr. Bastable, you're going to see some Cossacks, eh? A bit of the reality most Europeans miss." He dropped his voice and became sympathetic. "Does that bother you? The Steel Tsar rather than the Mikado?"

"Not a bit," I said. After all, I thought wickedly, I had originally been trained to fight Russians. But I have never been able to find consolation in cynicism for long and this lasted a few seconds. "Perhaps we'll find out if he's human or not."

Pilniak became serious. "He's human. And he's cruel. This whole thing is essentially medieval in its overtones, for all they claim to be socialists and nationalists. They want to put the clock back to the days of Ivan the Terrible. They could destroy Russia and everything the Revolution achieved. There have even been instances of pogroms in one or two of the towns they've taken, and God alone knows what's going on in the rural districts. They should be stopped as quickly as possible. But they're gaining popular support all the time. War brings out these basic feelings. They are not always controllable. Our newspapers beat the drum of Slavophilia, of nationalism, in an effort to stir up patriotic feeling against the Japanese—and this happens."

"You seem to speak as if this uprising was inevitable."

"I think it was. Kerensky promised us Heaven on Earth many years ago. And now we find that not only have we not made Heaven, but we are threatened with Hell, in the form of invasion. This war will leave many scars, Mr. Bastable. Our country will not be the same when it is over."

"The Steel Tsar is a genuine threat?"

"What he represents, Mr. Bastable, is a genuine threat."

CHAPTER THREE

Cossack Revolutionists

Yekaterinaslav was soon below us and it was obvious that the city was undergoing attack. We could see smoke and flames everywhere, little groups of figures running hither and yonder in the suburbs, the occasional boom of cannon fire or the tiny snapping noises of rifle-shots.

Yekaterinaslav was an old Russian-style city, with many of its buildings made of wood. Tall houses with elaborately carved decoration; the familiar onion-domes of churches; spires, steeples, several brick-built apartment blocks and shops near the centre.

On the nearby Dnieper river most of the boats were burning or had been sunk. Occasionally a ship, its paddles foaming the water, would go by the city and sometimes it would loose off a shell or two. Evidently these were naval ships commandeered by the revolutionists.

Pilniak knew Yekaterinaslav pretty well. He stood beside me, naming streets and squares. Some distance from the city, amongst demolished farmhouses and ruined fields, we saw the main Cossack camp: a mixture of all kinds of tents and temporary shacks, including more than one railway carriage, for the main railway line ran to Yekaterinaslav and much of its stock had been captured.

"That's it," said Pilniak in some excitement. "The Free Cossack Host. Impressive, you must admit." He raised binoculars to his eyes. "Most of their heavy artillery is further down the line, along with their armoured vehicles. They're saving up the cavalry for the final charge. There must be ten thousand horses down there."

"Not much good against airships," I said. "They look a pretty unruly mob to me."

"Wait until you see them fight. Then you'll know what cavalry tactics are all about."

As a matter of fact it did my heart good to hear someone using those terms. The last time I had heard people discussing cavalry tactics had been in the mess in my own world of 1902.

"You talk as if you're on their side," I said.

He paused, lowering his glasses, then he said seriously: "Everything free in the Russian heart is represented by our Cossacks. Every yearning we have is symbolized by their way of life. They are cruel, they are often illiterate and they are certainly unsophisticated by Petersburg standards, but they are—they are the Cossacks. The Central Government should never have imposed conscription. They would have volunteered in time, but they wanted to show that they were making their own decisions, not Petersburg's."

"This rebellion came about as the result of conscription?" I had not heard this mentioned in Odessa.

"It is one reason. There are many. Traditionally, the Cossacks have enjoyed a certain amount of autonomy. When the Tsars tried to take it away they always found themselves in trouble. They have large communities—we call them Hosts—which elect their own officers, their own leader—the *ataman*—and are very touchy, Mr. Bastable, about these things."

"Apparently," I said. "So in destroying this rebellion, you

feel you are in some way destroying your own sense of freedom, of romance."

"I think so," said Pilniak. He shrugged. "But we have our orders, huh?"

I sighed. I did not envy him his dilemma.

The ship had been sighted by the Cossacks. There was some sporadic artillery fire from the ground, a few rifle-shots, but luckily they had little or no anti-aircraft weaponry. The poor devils would be sitting ducks for our bombs.

The ship was turning slowly, heading for the airpark on the southern side of the city. Here we were to rendezvous with the other ships of the Volunteer Fleet.

Pilniak continued to peer through his binoculars. "Looks as if they're massing," he said. "They know they haven't much time now."

"They're going to try to take the city entirely with cavalry?"

"It's not the first time they've done it. But they have covering fire to some extent, and some armoured battlecars."

"Who's defending Yekaterinaslav?" I asked.

"I think we dropped some infantry a couple of days ago, and there's some artillery, too, as you can see. They were only sent to hold out until we arrived, if I'm not mistaken."

Now we could see the airpark. There were already half-a-dozen good-sized ships tethered at mast. "Those are troop-carriers," he said, pointing to the largest. "By the way they're sitting in the air I'd say they still had most of their chaps on board."

Even as he spoke the captain came on deck behind us and saluted us. "Gentlemen, we have our wireless orders."

We approached him. He was mopping his brow with a large, brown handkerchief. He seemed to be barely in control of his own agitation. "We are to proceed in squadron with three other ships, led by the *Afanasi Turchaninov*, and there we shall release our bombs on the rebel camp before they can move their horses out." He was plainly sickened by the statement. Whatever the Cossacks had done, however cruel they were, however insane in their ambitions, they did not deserve to die in such a manner.

His announcement was greeted with silence throughout the control deck.

The captain cleared his throat. "Gentlemen, we are at War. Those soldiers down there are just as much enemies of Russia as the Japanese. They could be said to be a worse enemy, for they are traitors, turning against their country in her hour of greatest need."

He spoke with no real authority. It would not have mattered a great deal if the horsemen were Japanese, it still seemed appallingly unsporting to do what we were about to do. I felt that Fate had once again trapped me in a moral situation over which I had no control.

Some of my fellow officers were beginning to murmur and scowl. Pilniak saluted Captain Korzeniowski. "Sir, are we to place bombs directly on the Cossacks?"

"Those are our orders."

"Could we not simply bomb around them, sir?" said another young officer. "Give them a fright."

"Those are not our orders, Kostomarov."

"But sir, we are airshipmen. We…"

"We are servants of the State," insisted the captain, "and the State demands we bomb the Cossacks." He turned his back on us. "Drop to two hundred feet, height coxswain."

"Two hundred feet, sir."

The grumbling continued until the captain whirled round, his face red with anger. "To your posts, gentlemen. Bombardiers: look to your levers."

Grimly we did as we were instructed. From the masts, which were now behind us, there floated up three other ships. Two positioned themselves on our port and starboard, while the leader went ahead of us. There was a funereal atmosphere about the whole operation. As he gave his orders, the captain's voice was low and bleak.

The wireless began to buzz. Our operator lifted his instrument. "It is the flagship, sir," he told the captain. The captain came to the equipment and began to listen. He nodded once or twice and then gave fresh orders to the helmsman. He seemed almost cheerful. "Gentlemen," he said, "the Cossacks are already charging. Our job will now be to try to break them up."

The task was hardly congenial, but anything had begun to seem better than bombing a camp. At least it would be a moving target.

CHAPTER FOUR

The Black Ships

I very much doubt, Moorcock, that you will ever know the experience of confronting a Cossack battle-charge, or, indeed, that you will ever witness it from the control deck of a sophisticated aerial cruiser!

Led by Admiral Krassnov's flagship, we raced lower and lower to the ground, to give specific accuracy to our aerial torpedoes. As we approached we were barely fifty feet up and ahead of us was a mountain of black dust in which were silhouetted the massed forms of men and horses. This, at least, felt more like a fair fight.

Standing on the bridge, peering forward, Captain Korzeniowski issued the command:

"Let go Volley Number One."

Levers were depressed and, from their tubes in the bow of the gondola, aerial torpedoes buzzed towards the yelling Cossack Host. The torpedoes made a high-pitched noise as the air was sliced by their stubby wings and then a deep-throated *boom* sounded as they entered the Cossack ranks. Yet for all they were inevitably deadly the torpedoes hardly seemed to make a scrap of difference to the momentum of the charge.

Next, as the riders passed below us, we released our bombs, lifting to about a hundred and fifty feet as we did so and then dipping down again to fire off another volley of torpedoes. The ship creaked to the helmsman's rapid turning and returning of the wheel, to the height coxswain's sure hand on his valve-controls. I've never flown in a tighter ship and as we did our bloody work I prayed for the chance of a real engagement with ships of equal manoeuvrability.

The Cossacks split ranks as we came down on them again and at first it seemed they were in panic. Then I realized they were tactical breaks to move out of our direct line of fire. They showed enormously disciplined horsemanship. Now I understood what Pilniak had been talking about. And, admiring such courage and skill, I felt even less pleased with myself for what I was involved in.

On a wireless order from the flagship we released the last of our bombs and went rapidly aloft. Now we could see the results of our attack. Dead and dying men and horses were strewn everywhere. The ground was pitted with craters, scattered with red flesh and broken bones. It was sickening.

Pilniak had tears in his eyes. "I blame that *staretz* for this— the mad priest Djugashvili. He's not a socialist. He's a lunatic nihilist, throwing away those poor lads' lives!"

It's common enough to transfer one's own guilt onto an easy villain, but I was bound to agree with him about the so-called Steel Tsar.

Not for the first time, however, I wished that the airship had never been conceived. Its capacity for destruction was horrifying.

On the bridge Captain Korzeniowski was pale and silent. He gave his orders in quiet, tense Russian. Whenever my eyes met those of one of my fellow airshipmen it seemed we shared the same thoughts. This could be the beginning of Civil War. There is no kind more distressing, no kind which so rapidly describes the pointlessness of human killing human. I have been fated, for a reason I cannot comprehend or for no reason at all, to witness the worst examples of insane warfare (and all warfare, it seems to me now, is that) and having to listen to the most ridiculous explanations as to its "necessity" from otherwise perfectly rational people, I have long since become weary, Moorcock, of the debate. If I appear to you to be in a more reconciled mood than when your grandfather first met me it is because I have learned that no individual is responsible for War—that we are all, at the same time, individually responsible for the ills of the human condition. In learning this (and I am about to tell you how I learned it) I also learned a certain tolerance for myself and for others which I had never previously possessed.

We had not managed to halt the Cossack charge, even though we had weakened it. As we returned to the airpark I saw the second stage of our strategy. On the outskirts of the city the larger troop-carriers were releasing their "cargo".

Each soldier fell from the great gondolas on his own thin wings.

In rough formation, the airborne infantry began to glide towards the earth, guiding themselves on pairs of silken sails to the ground where they reformed, folded their wings into their packs and marched towards the trenches already prepared for them. Next, on large parachutes, artillery pieces were landed and moved efficiently to their positions. As the Cossack Host approached the suburbs, it was met by a sudden burst of fire. I heard rifles and machine-guns, the boom of howitzers and field-guns.

Pilniak said to me: "I wish I was down there with them."

I merely wished that I was nowhere near Yekaterinaslav.

"Does the Steel Tsar lead his own charges?" I asked. Perhaps I was hoping that the man had at least died for his folly.

"They say he does." Pilniak grimaced. "But who can be sure? He's quite an old man, I gather."

"I wonder how a Georgian priest became a Cossack *ataman*," I said. "Doesn't that seem strange to you?"

"He's been in this part of the world for years. A Cossack is a *kind* of person, not a member of a race, as such. They elect their leaders, as I told you. He must have courage and he must have a powerful personality. Also, I suspect, he has the knack of appealing to people's pride. The Central Government has humiliated the Cossacks, who know that if they had not supported the Revolution, it would have collapsed. The Revolution started where our old uprisings always used to start, here in the South, on the 'borderlands' (that is what U-kraine means). It could have degenerated into pogroms and civil slaughter, but the Cossacks had been mistreated by the Tsar, used badly in the War against Japan, so they sided with the socialists and helped establish the first effective parliament, our Duma, which in turn caused Tsar Nicholas to abdicate. It was Cossacks who seated Kerensky in the Presidential Chair. It was Cossacks who put his picture in place of the Tsar's."

"You and your ikons—" I began, but Pilniak was in full, impassioned stride.

"Naturally the Cossacks feel humiliated by Kerensky. They gave him the power in return for their own autonomy. They see him as betraying them, as attacking their freedoms. On that day in October 1905 when he stood before the Duma and the representatives of all the Cossack Hosts, he spoke of 'eternal liberty' for the Cossacks. Now he appears to be making exactly the same mistakes Tsar Nicholas made—and is paying the price."

"You seem confused in your loyalties," I said.

"I'm loyal to our socialist ideals. Kerensky is old. Perhaps he takes poor advice, I don't know."

I looked back at the carnage, astonished that those wild, atavistic horsemen could have so much influence on the course of modern history. If it was true that they had only demanded their own freedom, rather than political power as such, then it was not surprising that they felt betrayed by those they had supported. There were many people who had shared their experience throughout history.

"Djugashvili promises them their old liberties back," said Pilniak bitterly, "and the only freedom he actually brings is the freedom of death. He's still a peasant priest at heart. Russia is cursed by them. They have something which the Russian people find hard to resist."

"Hope?" I said dryly.

"Once, yes. But now? Our country has almost universal literacy, a free medical service which is the envy of the world, our living standards are higher than most. We are prosperous. Why should they need a *staretz*?"

"They expected Heaven. You said so yourself. Your socialist Duma appears to have provided them only with Earth—a familiar reality, however improved."

Pilniak nodded. "We Slavs have always hoped for more. But until Kerensky we achieved far less. What could the Steel Tsar do for us?"

"Remove personal responsibility," I said.

Pilniak laughed. "We have never been fond of that. You Anglo-Saxons have the lion's share, eh?"

I failed to take his point. Seeing this, Pilniak added kindly: "We are still ruled, in some ways, by our Church. We are a people more cursed by religion and its manifestations and assumptions than any other. The Steel Tsar, with his messianic socialism, offers us religion again, perhaps. You English have never had quite the same need for God. We have known despair and conquest too often to ignore Him altogether." He shrugged. "Old habits, Mr. Bastable. Religion is the panacea for defeat. We have a great tendency to rationalize our despair in mystical and utopian terms."

I began to understand him. "And your Cossacks are prepared to kill to achieve that dream, rather than accept Kerensky's philosophy of compromise?"

"They are, to be fair, also prepared to die for the dream," he said. "They are children. They are Old Believers, in that sense. Not long ago, all Russians were children. If Djugashvili has his way, they'll become children again. Kerensky's mistake has always been that he has refused to become a patriarch—or, as you said, an ikon." He smiled. "Though he's come close in his time. Petersburg socialism seems cold to the likes of our Cossacks, who would rather worship personalities than embrace ideas."

I shared his irony. "You make them sound like Americans."

"We all have it in us, Mr. Bastable, particularly in times of stress."

The cruisers were nearing the masts now and making ready to anchor. Captain Korzeniowski reminded us of our duties and we returned to our posts on the bridge.

We were never to dock.

As the sun began to sink over the steppe, filling the landscape with that soft Russian twilight, Pilniak pointed with alarm to the east.

"Ships, sir!" he shouted to the captain. "About ten of them!"

They were moving in rapidly—medium-sized warships, black from crown to gondola, without insignia or markings of any kind, and as they flew they fired.

We had only our light guns and no bombs or torpedoes left. Before attacking us, these ships had evidently waited until we had spent our main fire-power.

One of the other cruisers received a terrific bombardment, so

heavy that it was knocked sideways in the air the moment before
its mooring cables linked with the mast. It made an attempt to
come up, nose-first, but explosive shells struck hull and gondola
with enormous force. One or two of its guns went off and were
answered by an even fiercer barrage. They must have hit fuel
supplies, for fire burst out in the starboard stern of her gondola.
She was holed, too, and jerking like a harpooned whale as she
dropped towards the buildings of the airpark, fell against a mast,
scraped down it and collapsed uselessly on the ground. Ground
crew ran rapidly towards her, preparing to fight the fire and save
her complement if they could.

Hastily Captain Korzeniowski ordered our gunners to their
various positions about the gondola.

"Whose ships are they?" I shouted to Pilniak.

He shook his head. "I don't know, but they're evidently not
Japanese. They're fighting for the Cossacks."

Captain Korzeniowski was at the wireless equipment,
conferring with Krassnov's flagship which, we could see, was
receiving a heavy bombardment. The black ships appeared
to single out one of our vessels at a time. He spoke rapidly in
Russian. "*Da—da—ya panimayu…*" Then: "Two thousand feet,
height coxswain. Full speed, minimum margin." This meant we
were going to have to hang on to our heads and stomachs as the
ship began to shoot upwards.

We clung to the handrails. As we climbed we also turned to
bring our larger recoilless thirty-pounders to bear on the black
ships below. It was a beautiful piece of airmanship and it was
rewarded almost immediately as we scored two good hits on one
of the leading enemy craft. Though my head was swimming, I
was elated. This was what I had joined the Service for!

Two enemy ships split away from the fleet and began to
come up towards us, but without the speed, the efficiency or the
sheer skill of the *Vassarion Belinsky*. We had little else, at that

point, but our superior airmanship, for we were outgunned and outnumbered. We continued to rise, but at a slower rate, still firing down on the two black ships which swam upwards, implacable and deadly, like sharks moving in for the kill.

We reached the clouds.

"Forward at half-speed," Captain Korzeniowski instructed the helmsman. He was very calm now and there was a peculiar little smile on his face. Evidently he preferred this kind of fighting, no matter how dangerous, to the sort we had first been forced to take part in.

"Cut engines," ordered the captain. We were now drifting, partially hidden by the clouds, inaudible to our enemies.

"Are we going to engage them, sir?" Pilniak wanted to know.

Korzeniowski pursed his lips. "I think we might have to, Lieutenant Pilniak. But I want to get us as much advantage as possible. Turn the main vanes two points to port, helmsman."

The ship began to come about slowly.

"Another two points," said the captain. His eyes were cold and hard as he peered into the cloud.

"Another point." We had almost made a complete turn.

"Engines active!" said Korzeniowski. "Full speed ahead."

Our diesels shrieked into life as we plunged into the open sky again. It was a grey limbo, with clouds below us and the darkening heavens above. We might well find ourselves fighting at night, using our searchlights to seek out antagonists. It would be a game of hide-and-seek which could last until dawn or even longer. Captain Korzeniowski was plainly preparing for this, attempting to buy time. By now our surviving sister ships would have attempted the same tactics. We had little choice, for we were all but helpless in any kind of direct engagement.

"Cut engines." Again we were drifting, waiting for a sight of the black ships. A wind was striking our outer cables, making them sing. Stars had begun to appear overhead.

Pilniak shivered. "It's as if the world's ceased to exist," he murmured.

In silence, we continued our drift.

Then we spotted them, below and about half-a-mile ahead.

"Engines! Full!"

Again our diesels screamed.

"Three points starboard, hard, helmsman."

We swung so that we faced the black ships side-on.

"Fire all guns!"

We offered them a broadside which was, in my view, a masterpiece of gunnery, sending a stream of shells in a vector towards both ships, which were sailing virtually side by side.

We hit one badly, evidently damaging its engines, because it began to turn in the wind, virtually out of control. We had no explosive shells and the enemy hulls could resist everything but a close-range total hit from our guns, so we were concentrating on their engines and their control-vanes. It was the best we could do.

The second ship began to go to cover in the lower clouds and now we could see that it was in wireless-telephone contact with its companions, for as the wounded ship withdrew, two more started to ascend. We could see nothing of our own sister ships and had to assume that they had taken evasive action or had been brought down.

The gondola shook violently and I nearly lost my footing as our hull received at least one direct hit.

"Rapid descent, height coxswain," ordered our captain.

We fell through the skies like a stone until we were actually below the enemy craft, slowing, it seemed to me, just before we struck the ground.

"Full speed astern."

We raced backwards over a deserted steppe. The city and the Cossacks were nowhere to be seen. Captain Korzeniowski had chosen his own area of battle.

The black ships were in hot pursuit, attempting to imitate our tactics.

One of the ships did not pull up in time. She hit the ground with a massive thump. Her gondola and all aboard her must have been smashed to fragments. She began to bump upwards again and we could see that she had left a great deal of debris behind. She was nothing but a drifting hulk.

Korzeniowski seized his chance. "We'll use her for cover. Get behind her if you can, helmsman. Forward, half-speed. One point to port."

Just as we swam in beside the ruined ship, her companion's guns began to go off. They hit the hulk and shells burst all over her, but we received only minor concussion. We moved up over her, all our cannon going at once and again we managed to damage vanes and engines on the nearest warship.

It was getting dark. Searchlights suddenly came on, blinding us as we stood on the bridge. Captain Korzeniowski gave the order to switch on our own electrics. It would make us visible to the enemy, but at least we would not be entirely blinded.

"Give them another broadside," said Captain Korzeniowski quietly.

Our guns sought the source of the searchlights and we saw the last black ship begin to retreat upwards, perhaps trying to lure us into pursuit.

Captain Korzeniowski smiled a grim, experienced smile and shook his head. "Half-speed ascent, engines slow astern."

We climbed away from our enemy, into the clouds again. I was mightily impressed by our captain's superb tactics.

Pilniak was elated, in spite of himself. "That's showing them what real air fighting's all about," he said. He clapped me on the shoulder. "What do you think, Mr. Bastable?"

I was not naturally capable of the same display of emotion as the Russian, but I turned, grinning, and shook him by the hand.

"I've never seen anything like it," I said.

The black ship had extinguished her searchlights and had vanished.

"We must wait until morning now, I think," said Captain Korzeniowski. "Thank you, gentlemen. You are an excellent crew."

The half-moon was now visible, seemingly huge in the sky. Again the captain gave the order to stop all engines. The Russians were cheering and hugging one another, absolutely delighted by what could only be considered a victory against almost impossible odds.

It was an hour or two later, as we rested and debated the morning's moves, as our operator attempted to get wireless instructions from Yekaterinaslav and then, when that failed, from Kharkov, that the ship was suddenly shaken by an almighty thump.

At first we thought we had been hit, but the ship was moving strangely in the air and had not descended a fraction. If anything, we had gained a little height.

We were asking ourselves what had happened when Captain Korzeniowski came racing from his cabin, glaring upwards. It was as if he, alone, knew what had happened.

"I'd never have believed it," he said. "They're better than I guessed."

"What is it, sir?" I asked.

"An old tactic, Mr. Bastable. They've been following us all along, using nothing but their steering gear to keep track of us, drifting as we've drifted."

"But what's happened, sir?"

"Grappling clamps, Mr. Bastable. They're sitting on our crown. Their gondola to our hull. Like a huge, damned parasite."

"We're captured?"

He grimaced. "I think it's more in the nature of a forced marriage, Mr. Bastable."

He shook his head, his fingers stroking his mouth. "My fault. It's the one tactic I didn't anticipate. If they get through our inspection hatches…" He began to issue more commands in Russian. Rifles and pistols were broken out of our tiny arsenal and a gun put into every hand.

"Everyone to the inspection hatches!" cried Pilniak. "Prepare to repel boarders."

I had never heard that phrase used before.

Above us the enemy ship's engines were shrilling now as we were borne forward.

"All engines full astern," said the captain. He turned to me. "It could rip us and them apart, but we have no choice, I fear."

The ship began to shake as if it was undergoing a gigantic fit.

Through the quivering companionways we raced for the inspection hatches, listening carefully, through the general row, and hearing noises from inside the hull which could only be men climbing slowly down towards us. To fire upwards into the inspection tunnels risked a gas-escape and the possibility of being incapacitated by the fumes. Fewer than half our riggers were issued with breathing equipment, for the *Vassarion Belinsky* had never expected to be captured by boarders.

"We're going to have to shoot when they emerge," said Pilniak. "It will be our only chance."

I held my revolver at my side, four or five armed riggers with rifles stood immediately behind me in the narrow passage as the ship shuddered and wailed in her efforts to free herself from our captors.

Pilniak said: "It was a daring move of theirs. Who could have guessed they'd try it?"

"They're as likely to destroy their own ship as they are ours," I said.

Pilniak offered me one of his wild, Russian grins. "Exactly," he said.

The hatch cover had begun to open.
We readied our firearms.

CHAPTER FIVE
A Question of Attitudes

In the dim moonlight entering from the overhead ports, it was impossible to identify the figures who first broke through. In Russian, Pilniak ordered them to throw down their arms or we should open fire. Then we noticed that they were waving a piece of bed sheet on a stick. A white flag. They wished to parley.

Pilniak was disconcerted. He told the invaders to hold their position while he sent for orders. One of the riggers ran back along the passage towards the control deck.

The men in the hatches appeared to be amused and made some cryptic jokes which I failed to understand and which Pilniak, it seemed to me, refused to hear. It was pretty obvious to me, however, that none of us wanted to fight in those close confines. Few could survive.

I think Captain Korzeniowski had realized this, for he returned with the rigger. Pilniak told him what was going on. He nodded, then addressed the man holding the white flag.

"You know that this is an impossible situation for both of us. Is your leader amongst you?"

A small, stocky man pushed forward and gave Captain Korzeniowski a mock military salute. "I represent these people," he said.

"You are the leader?"

"We have no leaders."

"You are their spokesman, then?"

"I think so."

"I am Captain Korzeniowski, commander of this vessel."

"I am Nestor Makhno, speaking for the anarchist cause."

I was astonished. Before I could check myself, I uttered his name: "Makhno!" It was the man with whom I had been imprisoned in Japan. I had never expected to see him again. I had no idea that he knew anything at all about airships.

He recognized me. His smile was cheerful. "Good evening, Mr. Bastable. You are once more a prisoner, it seems."

"You are not much less of one," I remarked.

He smiled. It was a quiet, sardonic smile, almost gentle.

He wore an old, elaborate Cossack coat, with a great deal of green and gold frogging, an astrakhan hat pulled onto the side of his head, a peasant shirt, belted at the waist, baggy trousers and high riding boots. He looked the picture of the romantic Cossack of fiction and I had half an idea that he deliberately cultivated this appearance. There was even a Cossack sword at his side and one hand toyed with the butt of an automatic pistol stuck into his silver-studded belt.

"You serve the rebel Djugashvili, I take it," said our captain. "Are you trying to talk peace terms?"

"I've given that up," said Makhno. "It doesn't appear to work. You mention peace and everyone tries to shoot you or jail you. I do not, as it happens, serve anyone, save those who elect me. But we have agreed to give Djugashvili our help during this campaign. We do not support his ideology, only the spirit of the revolution, the spirit of the true Cossack. We are anarchists. We refuse to acknowledge government or despots of any description."

"You'd not agree the Steel Tsar was a despot?" I said.

Makhno acknowledged my remark with a short bow. "I would agree absolutely. We believe neither in masters nor in slaves, Mr. Bastable."

"Merely in Chaos!" said Pilniak with a sneer.

"Anarchy means 'no government', not disorder." Makhno dismissed Pilniak's remarks as those of a naïve child. "And it has nothing whatsoever to do with Djugashvili's idiotic so-called socialism. We do not support him, as I told you. We support the spirit of the uprising."

Captain Korzeniowski was confused by this information. "Then how do we negotiate? What do you want?"

Makhno said: "You are our prisoners. We want no bloodshed. We would rather have your ship in one piece."

Captain Korzeniowski became stern. "I will not surrender my ship."

"You have little choice," said Makhno. He looked to the outer ports.

We all followed his gaze. On flexible steel ladders dangling from the black ship, armed men were clambering down towards our engine nacelles.

"In a few moments your engines will be out of action, captain."

Even as he spoke one of our screws stopped turning. One by one the other engines stopped. From outside, in the chill wind, came the sound of cheering.

The captain put his hands in his pockets and spread his legs. "What now?" he asked stoically.

"You will admit that you are completely in our power."

"I will admit that you are an expert pirate."

"Come now, captain. This is not piracy. We are at war. And we have won this particular engagement."

"You are a bandit and you have seized a vessel representing

the government of the Union of Independent Republics. That is an act of piracy, of rebellion, of treason. We are indeed at War, Captain Makhno. You will recall the enemy, I think. It is Japan."

"A war between authoritarian governments, not a war between peoples," insisted Makhno. "What sort of socialist are you, captain?"

Korzeniowski scowled. "I am not a socialist at all. I am a loyal Russian."

"Well, I am not a 'loyal Russian'. I am an anarchist and, as my birthplace seems important to you, a Ukrainian. We oppose all governments and in particular the Central Government of Petersburg. In the name of the people, Captain Korzeniowski, we demand that you surrender your ship."

Korzeniowski was in a dreadful position. He did not wish to waste the lives of his crew and he could not, in conscience, hand over his command.

"You are a democrat, I take it?" said Makhno.

"Of course."

"Then put it to your men," said the anarchist simply. "Do they wish to live or die?"

"Very well," said Korzeniowski, "I will ask them." He turned to us. "Gentlemen? Airshipmen?"

"We'll fight," said Pilniak.

Not one of us protested, but not all agreed. The idea of spilling Russian blood was abhorrent.

Makhno accepted this. Indeed, he seemed to have expected nothing else, yet he was not convinced. "I will give you a chance to debate your position," he said. He began to move back towards the hatches. "You cannot escape now. We are already carrying you to our headquarters. If any of you wishes to join our cause, we shall be happy to accept you as brothers."

Captain Korzeniowski did not order us to fire. We watched as the anarchists retreated, pulling the hatches closed behind them.

It was then that I realized we had been subject to a diversion. While we had parleyed, we had not given attention to what had been going on outside the ship. I think Korzeniowski understood this, too. It was obvious, as we returned to the control deck, that he did not hold a very good opinion of himself at that moment. As an aerial tactician he had no equal. As a negotiator he was by no means as successful. It seemed that Makhno (as I learned was his wont) had achieved checkmate without losing a single life on either side.

Helplessly, we watched the stars and the clouds go by around us as, with engines straining, the anarchist airship bore us steadily towards its base.

On the control deck, Captain Korzeniowski was sending a wireless message through to Kharkov, attempting to receive instructions and to give some idea of our position. Eventually, after several attempts, the operator turned to him. "They have cut our antennae, sir. We can neither send nor receive."

Korzeniowski nodded. He looked at Pilniak and myself. "Well, gentlemen, have you any suggestions?"

"Makhno has us completely in his power," I said. "Unless we attempt to reach his ship through our inspection hatches, we have no way of stopping him."

Korzeniowski bent his head, as if in thought. When he looked up he was in control of himself. "I think we can all get some sleep," he said. "I regret that I did not anticipate this particular problem, gentlemen, and that we have no orders to cover it. I think I had better say here and now that I release you from my command."

It was a strange, almost oriental thing to say. Again it gave me a better insight into the Slavic temperament than I had a few months before. I respected Captain Korzeniowski's attitude, however. He was a man of honour who believed that he had failed in his duty. He was now giving us carte blanche to act individually as we thought best.

In a sense I had been extraordinarily impressed by the exchange between Makhno and Korzeniowski. Both appeared, for all that they seemed to be in conflict, to have at root the same sense of duty to those they led. Once Korzeniowski had been proven, in his own eyes, incompetent, he no longer felt that he had any right to command at all. I had the feeling that Makhno and perhaps many of the Cossack *atamans* took the same view. Unlike so many politicians or military leaders they made no attempt to justify their mistakes, to cling to power. For them power held enormous responsibility and was merely invested in them temporarily. I was learning, I think, one or two things about the fundamental issues surrounding Russian politics—something which was not normally put into words by any side, by any observer. These issues were at once simpler and more complex than I had once supposed.

Pilniak was saluting. "Thank you, sir," he said. I had no choice but to salute as well. Korzeniowski returned the salute and then went slowly back to his cabin.

A notion suddenly came into my head. "Good God, Pilniak, he doesn't intend to shoot himself I hope."

Pilniak watched the departing captain. "I doubt it, Mr. Bastable. That, too, would be cowardly. He will resume command should we ask him. When there is something to command. In the meanwhile, he releases us so that we may take whatever actions we think will help us best, as individuals, to survive. We are a primitive people, Mr. Bastable, in some ways. Rather like Red Indians, eh? In a way? If our war-leaders fail us, they resign immediately, unless we insist they continue. That is true democratic socialism, isn't it?"

"I'm no politician," I told him. "I don't really understand the difference between one 'ism' and another. I'm a simple soldier, as I've said more than once."

I returned with Pilniak to our tiny cabin with its two bunks, one on top of the other. We slept fitfully, both of us having merely removed our jackets and trousers.

By dawn we were up, taking coffee in the mess. Captain Korzeniowski was absent.

A few minutes later, he joined us. "You will be interested to learn," he said, "that we appear to have reached the bandits' camp."

We all rushed out of the mess and up to the observation ports. The ship was dropping close to the ground. Trailing mooring ropes had been dropped from the hull. Even as we watched we saw a mass of Cossack horsemen racing towards the ropes. One by one they were seized by at least half-a-dozen riders.

In triumph, the Cossacks dragged our ship back to their headquarters, while Makhno's black battlecruiser let go its grapples and drifted some yards off, to fly beside us. We saw anarchists waving to us from their own gondola. I was almost tempted to wave back. There was no mistaking Makhno's feat. He was a very clever man, and plainly no fiery charlatan. I could make no sense of his politics, but I continued to keep a high opinion of his intelligence.

Slowly, ignominiously, our ship was hauled to the ground by the whooping Cossacks. These were evidently not the same men who had attacked Yekaterinaslav, but it was equally evident that they knew what we had done during the Cossack charge. I got a better look at them now. In the main they were small men, swarthy, heavily bearded, dressed in a mixture of clothing, much of it fairly ragged. All were festooned with weapons, with bandoliers, with daggers and swords; all rode wonderfully. They were plainly rogues but were not by any means mere bandits.

Soon our keel was bumping along the ground as the ship was tied to wooden stakes set for that purpose into the earth on the outskirts of a small, one-street town which seemed to have been taken over piecemeal by the rebels.

Our discussion soon concluded that we had best "play

things by ear" and avoid armed conflict if possible.

We stood there looking out at the Cossacks while they grinned and gesticulated at us. They did not seem to be threatening our lives. They were overjoyed with the capture of a Central Government ship and seemed to bear us very little malice. I mentioned this to Pilniak.

"I agree," he said. "It's true they don't hate us. But that's the last thing which will stop a Cossack from killing you, if he so feels like it."

I realized that we were in somewhat greater danger than I had originally thought. The Cossacks did not accept the usual conventions concerning a captured enemy and it was questionable now whether or not we should experience the next day's dawn.

Captain Korzeniowski remained in his cabin. As we stared out at our captors the tension in the gondola began to grow. Overhead we could hear men climbing over our hull, laughing and exchanging jokes with the Cossacks on the ground.

Eventually Pilniak looked at me and the other officers and he said: "Let's get this over with, shall we?"

We all agreed.

Pilniak gave the order to lower our gangways and, as the side of the gondola opened out, we marched in good order down the steps towards the Cossacks.

We had expected everything but the cheer which went up. The Cossacks are the first to acknowledge nerve when it is displayed as we displayed it. Perhaps Pilniak had known this.

Only Captain Korzeniowski refused to leave the ship and we accepted his decision.

Pilniak and I were in the forefront. As we left the gangway he approached the nearest Cossack and saluted. "Lieutenant L. I. Pilniak of the Volunteer Airfleet."

The Cossack said something in a dialect which defeated my imperfect Russian. He pushed his military cap back on his forehead, by way of returning the salute. Then he made his horse walk backwards, in order to clear a space for us, waving us on towards the village.

Still rather nervous of what the Cossacks might decide, on a whim, to do, we began to walk in double-file towards the rebel headquarters. Pilniak was smiling as he spoke and I returned the smile. "Chin up, old man! Is this what the British call 'showing the flag'?"

"I'm not quite sure," I said. "It's been a long while since I had occasion to do it."

The Cossacks, some mounted, some on foot, were crowding in on us. They were pretty filthy and many of them were evidently drunk. I've never smelled so much vodka. Some of them appeared to have dowsed themselves in the stuff. They offered us catcalls and insults as we walked between their lines and we were almost at the first buildings of the village when the press became so tight that we could no longer move.

It was then that one of our riggers, near the rear, must have struck out at a Cossack and a fight between the two began. Our carefully maintained front threatened to crack.

I think we probably would have been torn to pieces if, from our right, a horse-drawn machine-gun cart had not suddenly parted the ranks. One man drove the little cart while another discharged a revolver into the air, shouting to the Cossacks to desist.

The man with the revolver was Nestor Makhno.

"Back, lads," he cried to his men. "We've no grudge against those who misguidedly serve the State, only against the State itself."

He smiled down at me. "Good morning, Captain Bastable. So you decided to join us, eh?"

I made no reply to this. "We are heading for your camp," I said. "We accept that we are your prisoners."

"Where's the commander?"

"In his cabin."

"Sulking, no doubt." Makhno shouted something in dialect to the Cossacks and once more the ranks fell back, enabling us to continue on through the streets until Makhno's cart stopped in front of a large schoolhouse which flew the rebel flag: a yellow cross on a red field. He invited Pilniak and myself to join him and told the rest of our chaps that they could get food and rest at a nearby church.

We were reluctant to part from the crew and fellow officers, but we had little choice.

Makhno jumped from the cart and, limping slightly, escorted us into the schoolhouse. Here, in the main classroom, several Cossack chiefs awaited us. They were dressed far more extravagantly than their men, in elaborately embroidered shirts and kaftans, with a great deal of silver and gold about their persons and decorating their weapons.

The strangest sight, however, was the man who sat at the top of the classroom, where the teacher would normally be. He lounged forward on the desk, his face completely covered by a helmet which had been forged to represent a fierce, moustachioed human face. Only the eyes were alive and these seemed to me to be both mad and malevolent. The man was not tall, but he was bulky, wearing a simple, grey moujik shirt, grey baggy trousers tucked into black boots. He had no weapons, no insignia on his costume, and one of his arms seemed thinner than the other. I knew that we must be confronting the Steel Tsar himself, the rebel leader Djugashvili.

The voice was muffled and metallic from within the helm. "The English renegade, Bastable. We've heard of you." The tones were coarse, aggressive. The man seemed to me to be both insane and drunk. "Is it good sport, then? Killing honest Cossacks?"

"I am an officer in the Volunteer Air Service," I told him.

The metal mask lifted to offer me a direct stare. "What are

you, then? Some sort of mercenary?"

I refused to explain my position.

He leaned back in his chair, heavy with his own sense of power. "You joined to fight the Japs, is that it?"

"More or less," I said.

"Well, you'll be pleased to learn that the Japs are almost beaten."

"I am pleased. I'd be glad to see an end to the war. To all wars."

"You're a pacifist!" Djugashvili began to laugh from within the helm. It was a hideous sound. "For a pacifist, my friend, you've a lot of blood on your hands. Two thousand of my lads died at Yekaterinaslav. But we took the city. And destroyed the air fleet you sent against us. What d'you say to that?"

"If the War with Japan is almost over," I said, "then your triumph will be short-lived. You must know that."

"I know nothing of the sort." He signaled to one of his men, who went to a side-door, opened it and called through. Moments later I saw Peewee Wilson emerge. The Bore of Rishiri Camp back again as large as life.

"Hello, Bastable, old man," he said. "I knew there must be some decent socialists in Russia. And I've found the best."

"You're working with these people?"

"Certainly. Very glad to put my talents at their disposal."

The familiar self-congratulatory drone was already beginning to grate, after seconds.

"Mr. Wilson keeps our airships running," said the Steel Tsar. "And he's been very helpful in other areas."

"Nice of you to say so, sir." Wilson gave a peculiar twisted smile, half pride, half embarrassment.

"Good morning, Mr. Bastable." I recognized the warm, ironic voice immediately. I looked towards the door to see Mrs. Una Persson standing there. She had crossed bandoliers of bullets over her black military coat, a Smith and Wesson revolver on her hip, a fur hat pulled to one side. She was as beautiful as ever, with her oval face and clear, grey eyes.

I bowed. "Mrs. Persson."

I had not seen her for some time, since together we had inhabited the world of the Black Attila. Her eyes held that look of special recognition which one traveler between the planes reserves for another.

"You've come to join our army, I take it," she said significantly.

I trusted her completely and took her hint at once. Much to Pilniak's astonishment, I nodded. "My intention all along," I said.

Djugashvili seemed unsurprised. "We have many well-wishers abroad. People who know how much we have suffered under Kerensky. But what of your companion?"

Pilniak drew himself up and brought his heels together with a click. "I should like to join my fellow prisoners," he said.

The Steel Tsar shrugged. The metal glinted and seemed to be reflected in his eyes. "Very well." He signed to one of his men. "Dispose of him with—"

Makhno suddenly interposed. "Dispose? What are you suggesting, comrade?"

Djugashvili waved his hand. "We have too many mouths to feed as it is, comrade. If we let these survive—"

"They are prisoners of war, captured fairly. Send them back to Kharkov. All I wanted was their ship. Let them go!"

Pilniak looked from one to the other. He had never expected to be the subject of a moral argument between two bandits.

"I am responsible for all decisions," said Djugashvili. "I will choose whether—"

"I captured them." Makhno was cold and angry. His voice dropped, but as the tone lowered it carried increased authority. "And I will not agree to their murder!"

"It is not murder. We are sweeping up the rubbish of History."

"You are planning to kill honest men."

"They attack socialism."

"We must live by example and offer example to others," said Makhno. "It is the only way."

"You are a fool!" Djugashvili rose and brought his sound hand down on the desk. "Why feed them? Why send them back so they can fight against us again? Cleanse them!"

"Some will fight against us—but others will understand the nature of our cause and tell their comrades." Makhno folded his arms across his chest. "It is always so. If we are brutal, then it gives them a further excuse for brutality. By God, Djugashvili, these are simple enough arguments. What do you want? Blood-sacrifices? How can you claim to represent enlightenment and liberty? You have already been responsible for the slaughter of Jews, the destruction of peasant villages, the torturing of innocent farmers. I agreed to bring my ships to you because you promised that these things were accidental, that they had stopped. They have not stopped. You are proving to me as you stand there that they will never stop. You are a fraud, an authoritarian hypocrite!"

The voice within the helm grew louder and louder as Makhno's became quieter.

"I'll have you shot, Makhno. Your anarchist notions are a mere fantasy. People are cruel, greedy, ruthless. They must be educated to holiness. And they must be punished if they fail!" He was breathing heavily. "It is what all Russians understand! It is what Cossacks understand."

"You have no claim as a Cossack," said Makhno with a faint sneer. "I withdraw my help. I shall inform the people I represent and ask them if they wish to withdraw also." He began to turn away.

The Steel Tsar became placatory. "Nonsense, Makhno. We share the same cause. Send the prisoners to Kharkov if you wish. What do you think, Mrs. Persson?"

Una Persson said: "I think it would show the Central Government that the Cossacks have mercy, that they are not bandits, that their grievances are justified. It would be a good thing to do."

She seemed to have considerable influence over him, for he nodded and agreed with her.

Makhno did not seem completely satisfied, but he was evidently thinking of the safety of Pilniak and the rest. He drew a deep breath and inclined his head. "I shall assume charge of the prisoners," he said.

As he left with Makhno, Pilniak called back over his shoulder: "I wish you luck with your new masters, Bastable."

I only knew that my loyalty was to Mrs. Persson and that I had faith in her judgment.

When Makhno had disappeared, Djugashvili began to laugh. "What a silly, childish business. Was it worth an argument over the lives of a few goat-beards?"

Mrs. Persson and I exchanged glances. In the meanwhile, Peewee Wilson echoed the Steel Tsar's laughter. Neither seemed possessed of what I should have called a natural sense of humour.

"Is it true the Japanese are almost beaten?" I asked Mrs. Persson.

"Certainly," she said. "A matter of days. They have already begun to talk armistice terms."

"Then these people are doomed," I said. "There is no way that the Cossacks can resist the whole might of the Russian Aerial Navy."

Peewee had heard me. "That's where you're wrong old man," he said. "That's where you're very wrong indeed!"

I thought I heard Mrs. Persson sigh.

CHAPTER SIX
Secret Weapons

Later, when the Cossack chieftains had returned to their men, the Steel Tsar stretched and suggested that we all dine in the rooms upstairs. I had not had a chance to speak privately to Mrs. Persson and, indeed, had been cornered by Wilson who had told me how he had been picked up during the raid on Rishiri and "dumped" (as he put it) in Kharkov because he had "made the mistake" of telling people he was an engineer and they had needed engineers in the railway works. He had left the city soon afterwards and had been on a train captured by rebels. The rebels had brought him to Djugashvili and the revolutionist had taken a liking to him.

"He's got real imagination, old man. Unlike the imbeciles in London and Shanghai, who wouldn't give me a chance. All I needed was a bit of faith and some financial support. You wouldn't believe the inventions I've got in my brain, old man. Big ideas! Important ideas! Ideas, old man, which will shake the world!"

I found myself nodding, almost asleep.

"The Steel Tsar, old man, is giving me an enormous

opportunity to build stuff for him which will help him win the revolution. And then we'll have real socialism. Everything properly managed, like a well-oiled machine. Everyone will be a happy dog. You'll see. And all it will take is Peewee. I'm the key factor, old man. I'm going to be remembered in History. The Chief says so."

"The Chief?"

He indicated Djugashvili.

We followed the Steel Tsar upstairs. He had Mrs. Persson on his arm and was walking rather heavily, as if drunk. He turned back to me. "I had not realized you were friends. You will be able to help Wilson in his work, I hope."

"Certainly he will," said Mrs. Persson. "Won't you, Mr. Bastable?"

"Of course." I tried to sound as enthusiastic as possible, but the prospect of even another five minutes in Wilson's company was more, at that moment, than I could contemplate.

The room above was fairly bare, but a long table had been laid with wholesome Ukrainian food, including a bowl of red borscht on every place. Djugashvili seated himself at the top of the table, with Mrs. Persson on his right and Wilson on his left. I sat next to Mrs. Persson. A few moments later Nestor Makhno stepped into the room. It was obvious that he was a reluctant guest. He had another man with him whom I recognized. I began to wonder if Mrs. Persson had not arranged all of this.

The other man was Dempsey, whom I had thought killed on his way to a Japanese prison. He was pale and thin and seemed ill. Possibly the drugs had begun to poison his system. When he saw me he gave a crooked smile and came forward, lurching a trifle, though he was not obviously drunk. "Hello, Bastable. Very good to see you. Come along for the final battle, eh?"

"What?"

"Armageddon, Bastable. Haven't they told you?"

The Steel Tsar began to laugh that strange laugh of his. "Nonsense. You exaggerate, Captain Dempsey. Professor Marek assures us that everything is much safer now. After all, you took part in an experiment."

Dempsey sat down and began to stare at his borscht. He made no attempt at all to eat it. Nestor Makhno seated himself across from me. He seemed puzzled by me, perhaps surprised by the alacrity with which I had joined "the other side".

"It's a prisoners' reunion, eh?" he said. "Did you know, Comrade Djugashvili, that four of the people at this table have been prisoners of the Japanese?"

"So I gather." The Steel Tsar was opening a small plate in his helmet, to expose a mouth pitted with pockmarks.

Now I was prepared to believe the rumour that it was vanity which caused him to wear the ferocious mask. He began to feed himself with small, careful movements.

He turned to Makhno. "Did you deliver the prisoners to Kharkov?"

"Not personally. They are on their way."

"In padded railway carriages lined with silk, no doubt."

"They were sent in a cattle-train we requisitioned." Makhno knew the Steel Tsar was baiting him. He stroked his neat moustache and kept his eyes on his plate.

"For so cunning a tactician, you are lily-livered as a warrior," continued Djugashvili. "It would seem to me, comrade, that there is even a chance you are weakening our endeavours."

"We are fighting against the Central Government," said Makhno obstinately. "We are not fighting 'for' you, comrade. I made that plain when we brought in our ships."

"You brought your ships because you know you are not strong enough to fight alone. Your ridiculous notions of honour are inappropriate at this time."

"Our notions are never inappropriate," said Makhno. "We

simply refuse to rationalize murder. If we have to kill, we kill, in self-defense. And we continue to name it for what it is. We don't dress it up with fancy pseudo-scientific words."

"The people like those words. It makes them feel secure," said Mrs. Persson sardonically, as if to an intimate friend.

I wondered if she knew Makhno. It was even possible that he was a colleague. There was something out of the ordinary about the anarchist. Although the logic of his politics was beyond me, I was impressed by his recognition of fundamental principles which so many idealists seem to forget as soon as their ideals are rationalized in the language of political creeds. He carried within him a sort of self-control which did not deny passion and which, I thought, was almost wholly conscious, in contrast to Djugashvili, who relied on doctrine and masks for his authority.

Djugashvili continued to dig at Makhno.

"Your kind of individualism is an arrogant crime against society," he said. "But worse than that—it never succeeds. What good is Revolution when it fails?"

Makhno rose from the table. "It is proving impossible to enjoy my food," he said. He bowed to the rest of us and apologized. "I'll return to my ship."

There was a light of triumph in the Steel Tsar's eyes, as if he had deliberately engineered Makhno's departure, goading him until he had no choice but to leave.

Makhno looked enquiringly at Dempsey, who shook his head slightly and reached for his vodka.

The anarchist left the room. Djugashvili seemed to be smiling behind his mask.

Dempsey was frowning to himself as Makhno went out. Wilson began to babble about "rational socialism" or some such thing and for once he broke a sense of tension which nonetheless remained in the air.

A few moments later there came the sound of several pistol

shots from outside. There were footfalls on the stairs, then Makhno reappeared. His left arm was wounded. In his right hand was his revolver. He waved it at Djugashvili, but he was not threatening.

"Assassination, eh? You'll find at least two of your men shot. I know your methods, Djugashvili." He paused, reholstering his empty pistol. "The black ships leave their moorings tonight."

Then he was gone.

Djugashvili had half risen from his place, the light from the oil lamps making it seem that his metal mask constantly changed expression. The cold eyes were full of unpleasant passion. "We don't need him. He was attacking our cause from within. We have science on our side now. Tomorrow I intend to display Wilson's first invention to our men."

Wilson seemed taken by surprise. "Well, Chief, I think you might find it's not quite—"

"It will be ready in the morning," said the "Chief".

Dempsey had taken an interest in this aspect of the conversation, though he had hardly moved when Makhno had reappeared and made his declaration. Una Persson merely looked thoughtfully from face to face.

Djugashvili walked towards the door and called down the stairs, "Bring the professor up."

Mrs. Persson and Dempsey both appeared to know what was going on, but I was completely at sea.

Djugashvili waited by the door until a small man with greying hair and round spectacles arrived. He seemed almost as unhealthy as Dempsey. There seemed to be something wrong with his skin and his eyes were watering terribly, so that he dabbed at them constantly with a red handkerchief.

"Professor Marek. You already know Captain Dempsey. You have met Mr. Wilson. Una Persson? Captain Bastable?"

The professor blinked in our general direction and waved his handkerchief by way of greeting.

"Your bombs are ready, eh? And Wilson's invention is prepared." Djugashvili was swaggering back to his place. "Sit down, professor. Have some vodka. It's very good. Polish."

Professor Marek rubbed at his cheek with the handkerchief. It appeared to me that some of his skin flaked away.

"What sort of bombs are these?" I asked the professor, more from politeness than anything.

"The same as I dropped on Hiroshima," said Dempsey with sudden vehemence. "Aren't they, Professor Marek?"

"The bombs which are supposed to have started the war?" I said in surprise.

"One bomb." Dempsey lifted a finger. Mrs. Persson put a gentle hand on his arm. "One bomb. Wasn't it, Mrs. Persson?"

"You shouldn't—"

"That was experimental," said Professor Marek. "We could not have predicted—"

Suddenly I was filled with that same frisson, that same terrifying resonance I had already experienced, to a slighter degree, in Dempsey's company. I felt that I stared into a distorting mirror which reflected my own guilt.

In a small voice I asked the professor: "What sort of bomb was it that you caused to be dropped on Hiroshima?"

Marek sniffed and dabbed at his eyes. He spoke almost casually. "A nuclear fission bomb, of course," he said.

CHAPTER SEVEN

A Mechanical Man

Stunned by Marek's revelation, I could do little more than sit silently with my brain in the most profound and horrible confusion, as I tried to make some sort of sense, no matter how bizarre, of what I had just learned.

I tried to remember when I had first begun to feel some relief from the weight of guilt I had borne for so long. Had I experienced a kind of miracle? Had Cornelius Dempsey taken on my sin as his own? Had history been revised merely so that I should no longer have to think and dream of those millions I had helped destroy? Was all of this a singularly vivid hallucination, taking place in the space of hours or days as I lay dying of thirst in the ruins of Teku Benga?

No possibility seemed too strange. I stared across at the man who, in some terrible way, was my twin soul. Had the young anarchist who had introduced me to Korzeniowski at the Croydon Aerodrome subtly transformed the situation so that he, rather than I, steered the *Shan-tien* on her last mission to bomb the airship yards of Hiroshima? And were my adventures up to now merely a result of his success? Here was a future in which I was not responsible for that unforgivable crime.

So difficult was this idea to grasp in practical terms that I eventually gave up, forcing myself to listen while Djugashvili continued his egocentric monologues, his boastings and his diatribes. He made us drink with him. As a result, my anxieties were lulled but my confusion increased. He poured glass after glass of vodka into that little aperture which revealed his discoloured lips and he spoke of conquest.

He planned to conquer Russia first. Then the whole Slav world, both East and West, would eventually succumb to what he called "the justice of World Revolution". The Moslems and the Jews must also be controlled, he said, but this was more difficult. "They listen to different echoes." Often they did not respond to the same means of control as their Christian counterparts. He seemed to be telling us that while as an ex-priest, he had a fair idea how to manipulate the Slavs, he was baffled by other races.

"Finally," he barked through his food, by way of a joke, "there is always a solution to these questions."

Like so many fanatics, he possessed an appalling streak of timidity and terror which feared all that was not absolutely familiar. As his power increased, he would doubtless attempt to destroy anything that made him anxious. "In the lost childhood of Judas," said one of the poets of the Irish Empire, "Christ was betrayed." And what if Judas, not Jesus, had the power to shape history? What bestial monster would he make of human society? Was every demagogue, by definition, a Judas seeking to wrest the power of Christ from the world? Should we not always point the finger at such seekers after earthly power, no matter what their credentials or affirmations, and say to them: "By virtue of your calling you are our betrayer?" Bishop, politician, son of the people…

Perhaps, I thought, I had been too long in Makhno's company.

Again I glanced across at Dempsey. He was fairly oblivious of me and Mrs. Persson's attention was always elsewhere, though once she motioned me to silence, as if understanding the shock Marek's statement had been to me. Both she and Captain Dempsey appeared to be waiting something out, as if they had anticipated the evening's events.

For all my increased confusion, I also had the oddest sense that something in my brain—or at least my perceptions—was changing. All attempts to make logic of my situation were failing—*if* I insisted on logic as a fundamentally *linear* quality. Only when I let go, as it were, of these attempts did a kind of pattern emerge.

For a moment or two I saw myself as many individuals, each fundamentally the same yet, because of some small difference of circumstance, often leading radically different lives in radically different versions of our world.

Time and Space were the same thing. And they existed simultaneously. Only we who attempt to impose linearity on Time and Space are confused. We become the victims of our own narrowness of vision.

It is true we can manipulate Nature to a small degree, and make use of her benefits. But we could not create the wind which blows the sails or the electricity which powers the motor. Our natural animal instinct to use these elements makes us believe, in our folly, that we have some grasp upon existence, some means of turning the very stars to our own ends. Perhaps, through persistence, we could even do that. But we should still not have controlled the universe. We should merely have made use of its bounty.

Our attempts to manipulate Time and Space are like puny parlour tricks. They are impressive to the simple-minded. But what if Time and Space are merely as complex and subtle as our own brains? We have so far failed to understand one. Why should we believe we have the power to understand the other? And what if they are infinitely more complex than anything we can ever hope to understand, except perhaps through our technologies? Should we not content ourselves with putting our own little planet in reasonable order before committing ourselves to any larger plans?

Yet, I thought, as some peculiar kind of clarity emerged momentarily from my terror and drunkenness, a human creature *could* learn to exist in that uncontrollable environment where Time and Space merge and separate and swirl as one simultaneous thing. But how could one cling to one's own identity, knowing that an infinite number of other versions of oneself existed throughout the multiverse?

What was the quality which allowed Mrs. Persson, for instance, to move seemingly at will from this version of our history to that? Why was she not mad? And, if she were not mad, how might I discipline myself to survive the chaotic movements of the time streams? How did such people negotiate and map their environment? Were they nomads who followed certain well-tried trails or were they also subject to the random whims of a chaotic multiverse? How dangerously vulnerable was the linear world we had constructed for ourselves? It seemed squarely to depend upon the race's consensus to ignore the monumental evidence of the multiverse's divine disorder!

Another thought came: If I were not hallucinating, had I perhaps created this entire reality merely to remove from myself the guilt of so much murder?

Djugashvili's attention was suddenly focused on his empty bottles. He began to bellow at his servants, accusing them of drinking his vodka, of selling it, of trading it with the Jews and, when they denied this with abject fear of his passing mood, he beamed upon them and told them that it was the Jews who were hoarding the vodka and that some people should be despatched to make them give up what was by right the people's liquor. And he laughed openly at this hypocrisy, as if he were enjoying it for its own sake—as if hypocrisy and deceit were arts he strove to master in all their finesse and subtlety.

While the scene was taking place, Mrs. Persson turned and looked directly into my eyes. I felt a frisson through my whole body and I heard her speak, very quietly, to me alone.

"You are not mad," she said.

But Dempsey overheard her and looked up. "Unless the whole damned universe is mad." He gave his attention back to his almost empty glass. "Better ask von Bek about that."

Was von Bek alive here? Had he survived with Mrs. Persson? I wondered again how we had not been destroyed by the hell-bomb. Perhaps the very act of dropping the device had set off this great eddy of events—billions of new ripples across the fabric of the multiverse? The act had not merely been symbolic of mankind's cruelty and folly. It had resulted in profound metaphysical upheavals. Perhaps I was doomed to live one almost identical life after another until I found some means of understanding my part in that crime. Again, having received a glimmer of perception, I was plunged into stupefied bewilderment and had the presence of mind to pull myself together as best I could, if only to placate the unpredictable warlord. He had wandered back onto the earlier subject.

"Professor Marek! Marek! Wake up, you b—old p—!" he shouted to his tame scientist, who brought himself round with the alacrity born of long experience.

"Sir?"

"How many bombs did you say you had ready?" Djugashvili demanded to know.

Marek shrugged. "Four. All about the same strength, as far as we can tell."

"You are unsure?"

The professor was quick to deny any lack of confidence. "I have their measure now."

"So you can produce more quite easily?" his master asked. Light suddenly caught the steel of his helmet and made it burn like the face of some mighty fallen angel. It could have been the face of Lucifer himself. I felt then that he was perfectly capable of destroying the whole world without a shred of remorse if he believed that he could not, himself, go on living. Such creatures, I remember thinking, have always dwelt among us. They would reduce the multiverse to ash, if they could. Why, I agonized, can we not recognize them and stop them before they achieve so much power? A tiny part of the human race was responsible for the misery of the majority.

I thought again of the injustices which we ourselves casually perpetrated and I wondered how we should ever set anything to rights while we continued to allow such vast discrepancy, so much at odds with the religious and political principles we claim as our daily guides.

Such reflections were perhaps natural as I sat listening to Djugashvili's braggadocio, in which large notions of justice and equality were used to obscure the actuality of his ambitions. Professor Marek had plunged into a complicated explanation of his work which the warlord dismissed with a yawn and a wave of his hand. "Production, professor? Results. Can you produce more of the bombs?"

"Of course. With Mr. Wilson's help. The Yekaterinaslav laboratories had everything we needed. Our information was perfect."

Captain Dempsey lifted his head, but it was only to welcome more refreshment, brought from somewhere by the same trembling servants. Mrs. Persson did not seem pleased with his behaviour and her passing glance in his direction had only irony in it. She pushed her dark hair back from her face and I was struck once more by her refined beauty, her dignified bearing. She was the kind of woman a man of my sort, fundamentally a plain soldier, could only look up to. I could never aspire to win her. I doubted if any man would ever keep her for himself alone. There was a sense of freedom about her which nothing could hurt; even when I had seen her a prisoner of Major John in East Grinstead, about to be tortured, she had retained that same sense of integrity, reminding me of nothing so much as Sarah Bernhardt in her famous role of St. Joan. I think it was there, if not before, that I had fallen in love with her. Only now, as we listened to the bellowings of the grotesque beast seated at the table's head, did I realize how strong those feelings were. I would have laid down my life for her and, though I scarcely understood it, everything she stood for. Was she really Korzeniowski's daughter or was the old captain merely her mentor? Perhaps her lover?

She said: "I thought Yekaterinaslav was retaken."

Djugashvili shook his metal head and turned to glare with feigned good will upon her. "So it was. But we got what we were after. The purpose of the attack was to supply Professor Marek with certain materials and information he needed. At Yekaterinaslav they were working along similar lines to us, eh, professor?"

I felt suddenly very sick, physically ill and deeply tired. Yet I wanted to leap from my chair and beg them to stop talking so easily about those terrible bombs which, for all I knew, could easily destroy the entire globe!

How could Mrs. Persson hold her tongue? And what was keeping Dempscy silent? Why did they want me to say nothing of what I knew?

I looked from face to face and saw only fear. They were all as afraid as I! Even Djugashvili was appalled by his own god-like power. We watched as the knowledge dawned on him—through his vast drunkenness, his mighty self-appreciation—that he might well have the means of destroying the whole world!

By demonstrating this power, he could fulfill every nightmarish ambition at a stroke. He would be Emperor of the Earth! Everything and everyone would be at his personal disposal!

Djugashvili's lips moved beneath his mask.

His smile was almost sweet.

Suddenly Cornelius Dempsey was on his feet, supporting himself with one hand on the table. "You're wasting time, your honour. You'd better hurry up and use 'em, general. Otherwise the Central Government will be here to claim its materials back before you can make any worthwhile number of bombs. You'll have to put your money where your mouth is, old boy. After all, there's a huge aerial force on its way."

Djugashvili made an irritable, almost feminine gesture. It was one I had seen before, when some fact did not quite suit his dreams. His usual method was to ignore it or destroy it. "Certainly I shall use them soon, Captain Dempsey. It only needs one ship for our purposes, eh? And we have that now. That's why I was so glad to dispense with Makhno's services. He's troublesome and must be liquidated. No, no. We are saved, old comrade!" He became obscenely avuncular. "We have a ship. Captain Bastable—" he turned his medusa's geniality upon me "—we have *your* ship, the *Vassarion Belinsky*."

I felt bile rise in my throat. A thousand new, desperate associations rushed into my overcrowded mind. "Captain Korzeniowski would never fly her for you!"

"Captain Korzeniowski is no longer aboard. Indeed, his spirit is no longer aboard his body, Captain Bastable." The creature chuckled, deep in his chest, and he sighed. The air seemed suddenly full of the stink of sulphur and stale vodka.

"You killed him?"

"Naturally, as a non-participant in this very important game, he had to be set aside. He is no longer a functioning pawn, Captain Bastable." His eyes were now fixed on me and I was able to understand how he had been able to command so many so easily. I could not tear my gaze away from that awful glare. "*You* are lucky, Captain Bastable. You are still a functioning pawn."

It was his warning to me. He must have employed the same phrase a thousand times or more. He knew it to be effective.

But my life was of no value to me while such monsters as Djugashvili were allowed to walk free upon the Earth! Again I felt that strange frisson. Looking across at Cornelius Dempsey I saw his face change suddenly from that of a drunken, self-indulgent boor, to sardonic dandy and back again, all in an instant.

They were playing parts, the pair of them! Playing parts as hard as they knew, allowing themselves no relaxation beyond what they had both briefly permitted me. And the only reason they had slipped so swiftly from their roles was to demonstrate to me that I must act with them and reveal nothing. Yet I also understood from Dempsey that he, too, was playing for the largest possible stakes and was prepared to lose his very soul in pursuit of the greater good.

There is nothing which gives one strength at a time of need than the presence of comrades who share the same ideas about humanity and justice. Suddenly I understood how profoundly Cornelius Dempsey believed in fair play. Once, it had driven him to drink. Now he used drink to disguise the strange intelligence lurking within those deceptively drugged eyes. I understood that it was only the very best in us, our capacity for love and self-respect, that enabled us to survive in a perpetually fragmenting multiverse. Only our deepest sense of justice allowed us to remain sane and relish the wonders of chaotic Time and Space, to be free at last of fear. Further violence would bring only an endless chain of bloodshed and an inevitable descent of our race into bestiality and ultimate insentience. To survive, we must love.

I had not been listening while Djugashvili elaborated on this threat. My horror and loathing at his casual acceptance of mass-murder—including the wasted deaths of those who followed him—were almost unbearable. It remained difficult for me to understand how some people are simply born mentally deformed, lacking all the natural moral restraints and imagination which dictate the actions of most of us, however partially. Such creatures have learned from childhood to ape the appropriate sentiments when it suits them, to charm or bully their opponents, to agree to anything, to tell any lie and to pursue their own ends with implacable determination.

"Such men and women are the true aliens amongst you and it is ironic how frequently we come to rule you. We use your very best instincts and deepest emotions against you. We convince you that we alone can satisfy your need for security and comfort and then we drain you dry of everything save perpetual terror. Ha, ha, ha!"

I looked with astonishment at Djugashvili, wondering how he could possibly have uttered those words or known what I was thinking. His smile was a soft, deceiving thing lying upon the pitted surface of his head like a red slug. "Such monsters can only be murdered, Captain Bastable. Do you have the stomach for murder? Of course not. You will command the *Vassarion Belinsky*. Congratulations. You will become a hero of the people, a legend amongst the Cossack Hosts." He reached his irregular arms towards me as if to embrace me but then Cornelius Dempsey was on his feet, filled with unfeigned fury.

"No! This is treachery! That privilege was promised to me! You wicked old bandit, Djugashvili. It was all I asked of you."

The warlord turned from me to glare at Dempsey, his arms still outstretched. "Remember your manners, comrade!"

Mrs. Persson came to stand beside Dempsey. "Keep your promise, comrade. To me. You remember."

Djugashvili looked at her with honest disbelief as if any woman who trusted the word of a man was no more than a proven fool.

"You've developed a taste for mass-murder, too, Captain Dempsey," I said in a quiet voice.

The eyes he turned on me were no longer rational but were merry with a demon's light, the reflection of the steel mask. "Oh, yes, Bastable. Quite a taste for it."

Djugashvili seemed suspicious suddenly. Yet he kept to the original subject. "You will both command the ship. We must demonstrate our power to the Central Government, as we agreed. Therefore, we shall kill two eagles with one arrow and drop the first bomb on Makhno's camp. If the bombs are only partially successful and not strong enough to threaten the Central Government, we simply tell them we destroyed the rebels. We then make an alliance with them until we have perfected the bombs."

Professor Marek seemed offended at that. "There is nothing wrong with my bombs, sir! Everything will proceed as it should."

Djugashvili lifted a celebratory beaker. "Then let us drink to the total elimination of all who oppose us," he said.

"What a splendid idea," said Mrs. Persson.

Disbelievingly I looked around me for the source of an almost overpowering scent of roses.

We were forced to stay at the table while Djugashvili continued his monologues, mocking us for the weaklings he believed us to be, who scrupled too much to be able to kill him, who would obey him helplessly even when we knew he would eventually dispose of us, probably violently.

We were all involved in our own thoughts as we considered the future. I wondered if Dempsey and Mrs. Persson played their roles according to some agreed plan, or if they already improvised. Dempsey's anger had certainly seemed thoroughly genuine.

We let Djugashvili rave himself into incoherence until at last, without a word, he lumbered from the room, all unchecked ego and ruthless power, grunting for his servants.

"He's right, you know."

It was Peewee Wilson, his eyes bright as stones, deep in conversation with Professor Marek.

I was deeply weary but completely incapable of sleep. As I glanced towards our technological experts I saw a figure behind them in the shadows. He was a tall, gaunt man and his features were familiar. How had he come here? Mrs. Persson did not seem at all surprised.

"Von Bek," she said. "Thank God."

Events were becoming increasingly fragmented and dream-like and I wondered if we were not at that moment actually closer to the true nature of the multiverse. I also detected a hint of another kind of reasoning that better explained the actuality of our bizarre experience.

Von Bek was not the same anarchist nobleman I had originally met in my first adventure as a nomad of time, but I observed a strong family resemblance. Mrs. Persson introduced him as Max von Bek.

Von Bek was swathed in a long leather military coat. Beneath this was perfect evening dress. It looked as if he had completed his toilet only moments before. He spoke in a soft, drawling voice, slightly accented, and smoked small, brown cigarettes which gave off a sweet, almost herbal odour. The most remarkable thing about him was that he was a full albino, with crimson eyes and fine, aristocratic features. As he moved into the light this dramatic creature looked as if he had stepped from the pages of a glorious melodrama. "I am known in these parts as Monsieur Zenith," he said. "Here, a title and an old name are rather inconvenient." He held out his elegant hand and I shook it. "How do you do, Captain Bastable. There is some talk, I hear, of your joining us."

I did not follow him. A questioning look at Mrs. Persson caused her to smile. "We are already a little unsynchronized, Max. We're at present keeping some sort of course. We had a bulge in two sectors and almost lost a whole stability-zone, which we can't afford."

Her words were pretty much meaningless to me, but clearly Monsieur Zenith/von Bek knew what she was talking about. He listened soberly. Then he turned to me. "We think you'll want to join the League," he said. "In my view there is no better alternative for a gentleman faced with the stark evidence of the infinite multiverse, but you will be allowed eventually to decide for yourself."

I wondered what Peewee and Professor Marek were making of this conversation. When I looked at them I saw they were apparently frozen. I had an uneasy feeling. Had Monsieur Zenith actually arrested the flow of Time? I suppose he was amused by my expression.

"Time proceeds at many speeds and along many courses," he said. "There is the slow time of the trees and the brisk time of the mayfly, yet both perceive the flow from their own subjective viewpoint. Your companions arc currently experiencing mineral time, you might say, and merely appear to be completely still. Only a few of us, I must admit, have the necessary sorcery, as you might put it, to play these little tricks with Time." His manner changed suddenly and became very serious.

"We have no choice but to proceed with our original strategy if we are to save the maximum lives. We require a certain number of participants to play out the next stages of this game. If we lose, captain, there will be disastrous consequences for the human race and there is every chance that this sector will drag down all the rest. There is, in spite of what you might have feared, cause and effect in the multiverse and one sector can easily influence another. If we win, we shall perhaps do little more than preserve the *status quo*. Frequently it is all we can hope to achieve."

There was something in this foreign nobleman's manner, some authority about his vibrant voice and strange red eyes, that made me want to join my fate to his. Already I was prepared to serve in Mrs. Persson's cause, and if her cause were Monsieur Zenith's, so much the better.

For a second time I offered him my hand. "You can rely on me, sir," I said. "If Mrs. Persson vouches for you, I am at your service."

"Good man," said von Bek in resonant approval. "I am going to ask rather a lot of you, captain. I want you to play a part. In one sense it should be an easy one, for you must play yourself— but yourself before you grew aware of what you might call discrepancies in the fabric of Time. Am I making myself clear?"

"I think so, sir. In other words, you want me to go along with events just as if I didn't know any part of their outcome. I must follow my emotions, let Djugashvili and the others remain confident of their unchecked power…"

"Excellent." Von Bek nodded to Mrs. Persson. "You were spot on about this chap. He's the right stuff."

I flushed with embarrassment and pointed out that I was nothing but a simple British soldier doing his job as best he could in the service of the best cause he could find. "It's only what the Bastables have always done, sir."

"Then now you must do what the Bastables have always done and do it to the greatest of your ability," he said.

"I'm not happy with this tampering." Dempsey had revived himself. "What good will it do in the end?" He was still drunk and he looked at me almost jealously, I thought. He was a thoroughly wounded soul.

"You know better than I, old man," I said. "I'm pretty new to this sort of thing. You'll have to give me the appropriate advice."

"Don't patronize me, Bastable!" He turned away with a

shrug. "I'll help you. I'll help us all. And God help me." It was as if he were, as an actor, completely immersed again in his role. It occurred to me that members of this League were not always conscious of their situation, not always aware of any other existence, that a kind of saving amnesia affected them, allowing them to play out their parts with perhaps a little less anguish or, at least, uncertainty.

Von Bek offered me a sympathetic smile. "There's precious little personal reward in this work, old man. You have to be a bit of an idealist to do it."

"Then it's the job for me," I said.

He offered me a military salute, tipped an imaginary hat to Mrs. Persson, and returned to the shadows as Peewee said in offended tones, "I don't have to talk to you!"

Cornelius Dempsey chuckled and sat down next to Wilson, pretending a deep interest in what he was saying.

"You think we'll be able to blow poor old Makhno to smithereens, do you?" The drunkard was unmoved by Wilson's unwelcoming words.

"One bomb should leave a crater the size of the Grand Canyon," said Wilson in satisfaction. "We'll soon bring the world to her senses, old man. You'll see."

Dempsey's response was to place his head on his arms and return to snoring oblivion.

Mrs. Persson asked me if I would help get the man to bed. When we had laid him out on his bunk and left him as comfortable as possible we sat together drinking coffee in the tiny parlour. It was a pleasant house, full of painted fretwork and warm fabrics, and I wondered what *kulak* family had been killed or evicted in order to provide us with so much comparative luxury.

"Poor Dempsey's half-mad," said Una Persson, "and not always the most reliable ally. His judgment was destroyed and it's taken him ages to get to where he is now. For a long time he managed to keep himself going on a mixture of guilt and cynicism. A familiar enough combination. But now he sees an opportunity to put something right."

"How can we both bear responsibility for the destruction of Hiroshima?" I asked, hoping she would not warn me off the subject and make me return to my role. Some peculiar alchemy was already taking place, however, and my encounters of the last few hours had assumed the quality of a vividly recollected dream.

"Because we are all, in a sense, responsible for such great evils," she said. "Perhaps every individual member of the human race has had the experience you and Dempsey share. But that still does not remove your responsibility or mine. It is, however, a shared responsibility. We must all monitor our own actions. Our own actions can lead to something like Hiroshima, to the rise of Djugashvili. It is why we must be forever vigilant, forever attempting to adjust the Cosmic Balance. Every one of us should aspire, I think, to join the Just. That aspiration alone has a certain value."

I changed the subject. "I suspect you, Mrs. Persson, of engineering much of this, especially my encounter with Dempsey. This meeting of so many people connected with the first bomb— does it have something to do with your attempts to minimize the consequences of that event?"

"Time," she said, "will tell."

"At least tell me how Dempsey dropped a nuclear fission bomb on Japan."

"Similar circumstances to your own, Captain Bastable." She sipped her coffee. She looked exhausted and I felt that I was keeping her up, but she continued. "He's a socialist. He became idealistically involved with Chinese nationalists trying to get foreigners out of their country. At that time Professor Marek was also working for the Chinese socialists. They were the only people desperate enough to believe that he could develop such a bomb.

Other countries are working on the idea, of course, including the refining of uranium. That is what was going on in Yekaterinaslav. Like you, they had no idea of the power of the crude bomb they made. They intended to drop it on the airship yards—"

"This is too much!" I apologized for asking the question. "It is madness. It isn't possible." But I was by now convinced that it was all too possible for events to be experienced like echoes, over and over again, through all the layers of the multiverse, through all the flowing seas of Time and an infinity of material forms perpetually reproducing themselves.

Suddenly that scene aboard the *Loch Etive* came back to me. I recalled the faces of that other von Bek, of O. T. Shaw, of Mrs. Persson. A coldness filled me as I remembered the awful, blinding light rising to engulf us, my realization of the appalling crime we had committed. A crime, I had thought, without the possibility of redemption or restitution.

"They dropped it on Hiroshima," she said remorselessly. It was as if she was tempering me like a sword. Her words were hammer blows on the iron of my soul. "That's what started the war, as you know. It destroyed the entire city. Dempsey's vessel was his own. He'd put all his savings into buying it and going off to join the Chinese. It had a London registration. Of course, the ship had been sighted and the wreckage was easily identified—it had fused, part of it, into one solid sculpture. It was more than the Japanese needed. If there had not been a delay in the detonation, of course, nothing of the ship would have survived. Dempsey got out. As far as he knew he was the only one. The Japanese had wanted an excuse to go to War and now they had a moral crusade to boot. Everyone was preparing for War, anyway. The Japanese destroyed some British merchant ships. They didn't care. They were willing at that stage to destroy anything with a Union Jack on it and it's difficult to blame them. Well, of course, the British then declared War and the whole thing boiled over into the present mess. Dempsey was picked up by a Javanese freighter at first and only later did it dawn on him what he had done—what, indeed, he'd started. Poor devil."

I reflected that the Japanese had behaved rather well under the circumstances. "I know what it is to live with the deaths of millions on my conscience," I said.

Mrs. Persson gestured almost impatiently. "Oh, so do I, Captain Bastable. So do I."

I was deceived by the lightness of her tone. "It's a heavy burden for me."

"It's a shared burden, however," she said. "That was my point."

I was grateful for this comfort. Again my thoughts returned to the notion that Dempsey and I were shouldering the guilt for the same crime. Millions like us, perhaps, were also feeling what we felt. I groaned.

"You were both catalysts," Mrs. Persson told me, "no more than that. Do you still not realize your error? No individual can claim so much personal guilt. It is madness to do so. We are *all* guilty of supporting the circumstances, the self-deceptions, the misconceptions and misinformation which lead to War. Every lie we tell ourselves brings an evil like the destruction of Hiroshima closer. We drown in our lies. Hiroshima has indeed been destroyed in more than one world by more than one man, over and over again. The situations vary, but the people die just the same and in the same way. Some men feel they carry the whole weight of the crime. But we are all victims, Captain Bastable, just as in other ways we are all aggressors. At root we are victims to the comforting lies we tell ourselves, of our willingness to shift moral responsibility onto leaders, organized religion—onto a deity or a race, if all else fails. Onto God, onto politicians, onto creatures from other planets. It is always the same impulse, to refuse responsibility. If we do not take responsibility for our own actions, ultimately we perish."

"You share Makhno's views," I said. "Must one become an anarchist to join your League?"

She was amused by this. "It could be the other way around," she told me. "I have much in common with Nestor Makhno, however. I have the same skepticism of authority, especially when it is self-elected."

Somehow this conversation had relieved me. I lost much of my restlessness and uncertainty. I no longer felt such a helpless victim of Fate, though in some senses I remained one, quite as much as the unfortunate Cornelius Dempsey.

"Now we should sleep." Mrs. Persson got to her feet. "We don't want to miss Mr. Wilson's display tomorrow."

"Do you know what he means to reveal?"

"I think so, but I have left that whole aspect to 'Monsieur Zenith'. We each have responsibility for certain aspects of this affair, captain. I find that it rarely pays to anticipate events. After all, if they come as a surprise, one responds rather more spontaneously."

"I am still baffled," I admitted.

She put a finger to her lips. "Trust me," she said.

I would do whatever she required of me. "I will," I told her, "but I want no more innocent blood on my hands."

She picked up her cup and drained it. "If all goes well, Captain Bastable, we shall have completed our task here by tomorrow. Then you and I shall leave."

"Leave?"

"As you know, you have been invited to join the League of Temporal Adventurers. I would like to try to convince you that it is in your best interest—and ours—to do so."

"I shall listen to you, Mrs. Persson, and you know that I am at your service. However, I have some ambition still to return to my own time, my own world, where some kind of order at least seemed to prevail."

"Believe me," she said, "it did not last much beyond your time. You did not know it, Captain Bastablc, but whcn you were trapped in the ruins of Teku Benga, you also avoided the experience of Armageddon in your own world. Nothing is free of this terrible *wrongness*, this bestial violence, this destructive machismo. Oh, I cannot tell you how weary one becomes of it. You must reconcile yourself to the fact, my dear friend, that you will never know that innocence and security again. It was an illusion. Security is hard-earned and never maintained by violence, even the violence you employed as a servant of your Empire. You cannot return to your own time. The League offers you a home and a purpose, a chance to take a little control of your own fate."

I accepted what she said without question, but it was not palatable.

"In the meanwhile," she told me, "please continue to follow my lead. This is a very complicated business indeed, captain. A circle must be completed. A certain marriage must take place. A job," she grinned suddenly, in self-mockery, "must be done."

Next morning we were all called to assemble outside the school, in the large quadrangle behind the main building. Cossacks were coming and going everywhere. The entire camp was busy with the rattle and rumble of horses and soldiers, artillery and heavy vehicles. In the distance the armoured trains went by, loaded with men and armaments. Everyone had heard that Yekaterinaslav had been recaptured, that the Japanese were suing for peace and that Central Government troops, no longer busy with one enemy, were on their way to put down this unruly uprising before it expanded into fully-fledged Civil War. The Centralists, of course, had no notion of the kind of armament Djugashvili brought against them.

He strutted before his *atamans*, full of brassy confidence and comradely reassurance, a Cossack among Cossacks, a man amongst men. "Have no fears, my friends. This attack will be easily resisted. And very shortly Moscow will be suing for peace. We shall be at the very gates of Petersburg and those bloodless weaklings, those aliens who seek to control our fate, will be kneeling and kissing the hoofs of our horses!"

One handsome old *ataman*, splendid in black and silver, tugged at his great, grey beard and grumbled. "The airships will blow us to bits. They are cowards. They will not engage us honourably. We can't get at them. Cossack courage is useless against them."

"We have Cossack science," the warlord promised. "Our own superior science, untainted by their vice and weakness. Our science will easily wipe out the threat of their ships." The steel mask glinted as he raised his eyes towards the pulsing sun. "You will see. Within a week we shall be stabling our horses in the Hermitage—if we have allowed the Hermitage to remain."

The *ataman* became nervous. "By God, *hetman*, I hope you'll use no Devil's magic. I am an honest Christian…"

"We fight for God and Socialism," Djugashvili reassured him. "For the Freedom of the Great Cossack Host. God has put an instrument into our hands which will ensure our freedom for all time, and will enable good socialists to do His work. It is Christ whom we serve, my friend. Christ against the evil forces of Anarchy!"

The old Cossack seemed to accept this and nodded. Again I was forced to make sure my incredulity did not show on my face. I tried to avoid Mrs. Persson's sardonic eye.

"For God and Socialism," she murmured. "And we shall destroy all who stand against them."

But the mollified *ataman* was striding away on his bowed legs, glad to get back to his pony and swing up into the saddle. He rode away to give his men the news.

Mrs. Persson murmured to me in English: "It's in the nature of a good despot to say anything that will convince someone to do as he wishes. Only when he does not need them does he really say what he thinks. And by that time, of course, because he has no need of them, they are usually as good as dead. The secret of becoming a successful tyrant lies in an early ability to be all things to all people."

"You sound as if you'd trained him yourself," I said.

She made to reply but instead began to button her military coat. She had seen Djugashvili striding up behind me. He stopped as I turned to confront him and his burning eyes fixed me. "Where's our Captain Dempsey?" he asked. "He seemed so anxious to take command of the ship. Is he fit enough for it, do you think? If not, you will have sole command, Bastable."

"I would be glad of that," I said. "It is some time since I had full command of an airship. But I think Dempsey is ready for the job."

I had seen my alter-ego that morning. It was pretty obvious that he was sustaining himself on drugs. He had, however, been absolutely determined to captain the *Vassarion Belinsky*. He had asked us to go ahead of him. He had promised to join us shortly.

Djugashvili offered his back to me, idly rubbing at his steel helmet as if it were a real face. I wondered if he had slept in it. "He had better be in control of himself." His manner was crudely threatening. "Good morning, Mr. Wilson."

Peewee Wilson appeared, walking ahead of a dozen Cossacks who were carrying some massive object on their shoulders. The thing was wrapped in a mixture of canvas and sacking and was about twice as long as a tall man.

"You're ready for us, eh?" Djugashvili became jocular,

almost excited, like a spoiled boy involved with the prospect of a new toy.

Wilson seemed ill at ease. "Morning, Chief. I hope—"

"So do I, Mr. Wilson. Our pride and joy is about to perform, I presume."

"Oh, yes, Chief. There are no major problems."

"We want no problems at all, Mr. Wilson." It seemed as if the Steel Tsar was goading his creature, amused by his mixture of nervousness and fanaticism, yet at the same time not wanting to be disappointed by whatever it was he had commissioned from the English mechanic.

"This is what we need for our morale," Djugashvili informed us confidently. "Mr. Wilson has the measure of our Cossack lads. He knows what impresses them. Have you heard the news, by the way?" he chuckled. "Enemy scouts have already been sighted in the air to the south and the west."

"Well, Chief, I hope… I mean, we're ready, of course. Just the ticket for our War Effort, eh?" Wilson's own attempt at mirth was chilling. "Perhaps if we had a private demonstration first…"

"Nonsense, Mr. Wilson. I have every faith in you. This is what we need to rally our boys. We have to show them that our science is not only superior but also more familiar. This will bring their legends to life. They are sustained by legends, these people. It is their substitute for reason, believe me." His contempt for those he used suddenly came to the surface and he checked himself. He could not afford to lose a single Cossack regiment at this stage. He seemed to become impatient with himself and again made a strange little gesture. He began to walk backwards, signaling for the men to bring the huge object into the centre of the quadrangle and motioning for the watching Cossacks to stand back. They were a colourful mixture in their bright kaftans and uniforms, with their swinging swords and bandoliers glinting in the morning light.

Djugashvili positioned himself in the centre of his captains and called to Peewee Wilson, who still seemed uncertain of what he was supposed to do. He directed the men to lower the object to the ground and then, using ropes, raise it to an upright position. After further hesitation, he began to pull at the rags swathing it. It looked like a huge Egyptian mummy, clad in unsanitary winding cloths.

"Come, come," Djugashvili called. "Do not be modest, Mr. Wilson. Let us see your scientific miracle, the proof of our superiority! Captain Bastable and Mrs. Persson are clearly very curious to know what we have invented between us."

Suddenly, with rapid, almost desperate movements, Wilson began to tear at the canvas and sacking. The thing was made entirely of metal but only as he stripped away the last of the coverings did we see what it was—a gigantic human figure made entirely of steel and wearing, in metal, the regalia of a Cossack *hetman*.

Djugashvili began to laugh uncontrollably. "Isn't he fine? Isn't he an inspiration? So muscular and strong. So handsome."

Neither Mrs. Persson nor myself could respond. We were struck dumb by the idolatry, the sheer egomaniacal obsession, of the warlord as he strutted up to the figure and stared into its gigantic features, which were identical, in every way, to the mask which rested upon the head of Djugashvili—one steel face peering up into another. This sense of mirrors distorting infinitely the very substance of the multiverse was very strong and I found myself looking for Dempsey, my own strange twin.

Peewee Wilson the English mechanic had produced an image of the self-proclaimed *hetman* that was more than twice life-size. It gave me the impression that Time was coagulating or perhaps deliquescing. Somewhere, I thought, I heard a bass drone. I looked to the sky but saw nothing.

"Isn't he magnificent?" Djugashvili was swollen with pride,

strutting about the thing as if he already believed the great steel giant to be himself.

"He is splendid," said Mrs. Persson.

The best I could do was pretend to nod enthusiastically. I still could not find words to describe my reaction to this extraordinary exercise in egocentricity.

"This is only the first," Djugashvili told us. "Soon there will be a Steel Tsar overseeing every town. To remind them of their master, that it is through his will and his alone that they live. This mighty hero will lead the Cossacks into battle. He will show himself to be invulnerable. He will represent all that is best in me!"

"When do you intend to employ him?" Mrs. Persson watched as Peewee Wilson proudly polished his creation's left knee.

"At once. He will help distract the Central Government forces while you, Captain Bastable, will fly the ship to Makhno's camp and drop the first bomb. I presume he is ready to march, Mr. Wilson?"

"Oh, yes, Chief. Certainly, Chief." Wilson took an oil can from the pocket of his green overalls and applied a drop or two to the joints he could reach. He seemed to be taking as much time as he could, perhaps wishing to delay the moment, as if his own faith in his invention were not quite as strong as his master's.

Djugashvili turned to the *atamans*. "Now, my comrades, go and assemble your riders. Bring them here and we shall demonstrate the invulnerable power of the Steel Tsar! The first of the great army of mechanical men who will carry our banners across the world!"

"Just the ticket, old boy." It was Dempsey. Already apparently drunk, he had had a shave. His neat airshipman's uniform was a little too big for him. He was haggard but he walked steadily, and for all his slightly inebriated air he seemed to have lost the despairing attitude I had begun to identify with him. He even winked at me as he turned up. "Morning, Bastable. Ready to go aloft?"

"We're all ready, I think," said Mrs. Persson. "Hello, Professor Marek. Did you oversleep?"

The scientist was distracted. He looked the great steel statue all over and shook his head. "Not yet," he mumbled. "Too soon. Far too soon." He barely acknowledged her greeting. He tugged at his ear nervously, threatening to tear it off. Like us, he fell in behind our Chief as Djugashvili walked rapidly across the quadrangle to where a rough-and-ready dais had been erected. We were supposed to join him on this. Meanwhile, there was dust rising on all sides as the Cossack horsemen rode in an ever-tightening circle to attend the gathering called by their *hetman*. Those wild riders in all their savage finery were, in spite of everything they stood for, one of the most colourful and thrilling sights in the world.

Mrs. Persson offered me a small pair of powerful field-glasses she carried and I stood on the platform, watching the Cossacks coming in. They had not left their armoured vehicles or their artillery behind. As they reached the school, they fired off their carbines in salute and Djugashvili returned their greeting with a fatherly wave.

Peewee Wilson was running round and round the great steel figure checking every part of it. He seemed a little more relaxed now, as if he was confident his invention would not disappoint his Chief.

Now the Steel Tsar lifted his arms and addressed the great mass of his followers, his voice amplified by some natural echo, so that all could hear it.

"Free Cossacks." he cried, "Your blood has been spilled in the holy cause of Liberty and Socialism. The Central Government has sent her might against us. All the powers of her science are being brought to bear upon the Cossacks. They would destroy us forever. They would make Cossack history mere folk tales and the great noble deeds of the Hosts turned into comic stories. Such dishonour is impossible to contemplate, impossible to tolerate. But now we have our own pure science, untainted by their alien blood! We can create our own miracles! Behold!"

His pointing finger focused thousands of pairs of eyes upon the dominating figure of the metal man which rose to the school's roof and which could be seen from all sides.

"Here is a Tsar made truly of steel. He is an impregnable battle-leader worthy of the Free Cossacks. He will lead you against anything the enemy can muster. He is the symbol of all I stand for. He will bring inevitable victory."

A great cheer went up from the Cossacks. Sabres whistled from their scabbards and burned like brands in the morning air. These men were always impressed by such flashy symbolism. Djugashvili had got their measure well and Wilson had been able to translate his ideas into reality.

"Now, comrade—" Djugashvili turned to his tame mechanic "—now you must give life to our new leader. You must set him in motion. You must demonstrate his magical power!"

Self-controlled at last, Wilson reached up to the figure's waist and depressed a small lever. He stepped hastily backward, almost tripping, as slowly the steel creature began to come to life.

Wilson seemed to detect an unfamiliar movement in the mechanical man and frowned. I recalled that the albino Count von Bek had taken an interest in Wilson's invention. Had that mysterious visitor made any adjustments of his own to Wilson's marvel…?

Again the mechanic relaxed. Smoothly his giant seemed to respond to a grandiose gesture of the warlord's and with awkward, spastic movements, reached to its belt and drew its huge sabre, a match to its scale. With a screech the sabre cleared the scabbard and again the Cossacks cheered.

They were mightily impressed. Djugashvili had gauged their needs well. They were all cheering as the mechanical man raised the sword over his head. Again they waved their own sabres in response. They made their horses rear and buck. The noise of their approval was deafening.

Slowly the monster turned its head, as if listening. It inclined its gaze to stare down at Wilson. It lifted its head again. It seemed to be peering from one figure to the other, from the dais to the assembled Hosts.

Evidently these movements had been part of a programme already designed by Wilson and approved by Djugashvili. I had never seen the warlord more puffed up or pleased with himself. Already, in his mind, he ruled the world.

Mrs. Persson began to applaud. Her cue was taken up by the rest of us, to Djugashvili's further immense approval. Ponderously he, too, began to clap his hands together.

Mrs. Persson put her lips close to my ear. "He loves public adulation as much as his Cossacks love ikons. They would rather admire statues than real people. It has been their undoing for centuries."

Dempsey had begun to laugh, almost uncontrollably, and only grew silent when Mrs. Persson signed to him to stop. I, for my part, found the whole scene nightmarish. Dempsey cast a bloodshot, crazy eye about him and then, chillingly, winked at me.

As if in imitation of the cheering Cossacks, the mechanical Tsar now waved its sabre over its head. Wilson had recovered his confidence entirely. He had the air of a ringmaster in charge of an especially fierce beast. He bowed and strutted, a great, broad grin on his face and, for that moment, I saw something in him that I could like. The man was happy. He was doing what he had always dreamed of doing. He was proud of his accomplishment. All his whining and pontificating, his groveling and bullying, his greedy ambition, had been expressions of a profound disappointment, a loss so terrible to him, I guessed, that he could never recall exactly what it was that had been taken away. And now, in these dreadful circumstances, at the behest of a pathological mass-murderer, in a remote part of the Russian Empire, Peewee Wilson had come into his own. This was his moment. He might have been a matador swaggering before the Spanish crowd, a matinee idol standing before his admirers, a general returning from a victorious campaign. The applause, as far as he was concerned, was all for him. He reached to set another lever.

The steel giant began to lumber forward again, heading towards the dais.

It stopped in mid-stride. Then one of its knees bent a little so that it seemed he stumbled and might fall. Djugashvili looked a little apprehensive as the thing loomed over us, but he continued to clap, even when a grinding screech issued from the knee joint as the giant swayed.

I think Wilson had meant the mechanical creature to fall upon one knee in a gesture of supplication to Djugashvili but the motion had been halted and the Steel Tsar thrown off balance. The knee jerked two or three more times. There was the squeak and the clash of metal again. The monster began to turn, but its leg still dragged. It swayed again and this time we flinched, certain it must fall on us. Djugashvili flung up his arm and I could have sworn I heard him whimper. Only as the thing swayed away in the opposite direction did he recover himself and it was obvious to us all that he was vastly angry at being forced to show his fear.

He leaned over the dais, letting out a stream of disgusting language in Russian and then a further torrent in which I took to be his native Georgian. There followed more expletives in English and French, all of them directed at the unfortunate Wilson, who saw his whole moment of triumph fading away to be replaced by the threat of unusually painful death.

"Set the thing to rights, Wilson, old man, for God's sake." Cornelius Dempsey was the only one of us who seemed amused.

Djugashvili's voice was venomous. "Make him behave, Wilson. Or must I first teach *you* to behave?"

Wilson was in no doubt about the nature of the threat. He ran towards his creation, reaching up towards its waist, grabbing for other levers.

"Please," he was whimpering. "Please." He seemed to be begging the mechanical man to obey and pleading for his life at the same time.

The whole scene sickened me. I pressed forward to beg the warlord to stop this farce. I could not bear to see even as unlikable a creature as Wilson humiliated in this way. But Mrs. Persson made me pause. I knew there was no way I could influence Djugashvili. It was like being forced to watch in silence while a man beat a dog.

Blindly, Wilson tugged at levers and all at once the giant straightened up. He fell back, grinning with relief, casting a wild glance towards his master. His chest rose and fell, his unhealthy skin shone with his terror. He was close to collapse and yet gibbering in his gratitude for his escape.

But now he fell silent, looking up at his creature as it appeared to peer down at him.

The Cossacks had stopped cheering. The whole vast Host was hushed and those of us on the dais moved forward, also silent.

It was as if the air were filled only with the sound of Wilson's erratic, terrified breathing. His placatory grin towards the dais had no hope in it. Djugashvili's mouth seemed to move in a grimace of hellish amusement and then he flung back his metal head and began to laugh.

None joined him.

Marek muttered something about the levers and made to descend the steps, but Djugashvili stopped him with the flat of his heavy, peasant hand. "This is entertaining. Let us see what happens."

"The levers are wrongly placed. I can see it from here. They are in different coloured metals…"

"No matter, no matter. Wait." Again Djugashvili chuckled. "Watch."

The great steel warrior was moving again. The sword arm rose higher, inch by creaking inch.

Wilson took a step backward. Then he took another. Suddenly a sound like the roar of Babel issued from the metal mouth. It was as if every member of the human race gave voice at once.

Wilson covered his ears, screaming. "No!" He shook his head. "That's wrong. It's wrong. I didn't!"

The voice swelled again from the metal throat. It was unbearable.

"Can't you stop the thing, Marek?" I asked the scientist, but he shook his head, gestured towards his master and shrugged.

Wilson stumbled away. Now the giant moved in two long strides to stand over him as, in his uncontrollable fear, he fell to the dust of the quadrangle.

"This wasn't how it was supposed to be!" Wilson's scream was, to my ear, almost the scream of a betrayed child. I still remember it. I have never heard a sound like it.

Then, with swift inevitability, the sword began to descend. Wilson's scream was suddenly stilled.

The sabre had sliced him from crown to breastbone. His blood rained upon the canvas of the dais, upon Djugashvili and Marek, who craned forward now.

Wilson's body collapsed like butcher's meat into the dust.

Dempsey began to cough. It was a dry, hard noise, echoing in the silence.

Not a Cossack voice was raised. There was still an air of expectancy as they waited to see what either of the Steel Tsars would do next. I heard the wind sighing over the steppe.

Then, with a speed which shocked me, the creature fell with a grinding of cogs and wheels down upon its creator's corpse until all we saw of poor Peewee Wilson were his carefully polished boots.

Professor Marek was saying to his master: "It was too soon, comrade. He didn't give himself enough time. He was too hasty. The levers were in the wrong places. It is very important where they…"

Djugashvili clapped the scientist on the back and again his brutal laughter filled the air.

"Well, well. This is poetry, professor. What poetry! The stuff of epics, eh. Very well arranged. Excellent." He was praising Marek, I think, for Wilson's murder. In this way he made the man his ally in evil. Marek could neither deny nor agree. He left the dais and began to cross the square, heading towards the fallen giant and the crushed figure which lay beneath it. He approached uncertainly, as if he feared the thing would come alive again and turn its fury upon him.

Djugashvili was addressing his Cossacks again, his arm raised in a triumphant salute. "The traitor Wilson has paid the price of his treachery! It is fine justice that he is the first to die beneath the vengeful sword of the Steel Tsar! Comrades, the foreigner was a spy for the Central Government. He planned, in his cunning, to sabotage our War Effort. But we anticipated his plans and punished him, for the Steel Tsar obeys only its true master, your *hetman*! We are revenged, brothers! Freedom! Freedom!"

"Poor Wilson," said Una Persson. "What a dreadful lesson."

"And a final one," said Dempsey. His body was still convulsing. He moved away.

Djugashvili turned to us. "We are all rid of a bore, eh?" He chuckled, calling to the scientist, who had reached the fallen giant. "Revive him, Professor Marek. Get him back to the laboratories. He must lead our troops tomorrow."

Marek fiddled expertly with the thing, unscrewing levers and putting them in different parts of the mechanical creature's machinery. Who had tampered with the levers? Not Marek himself, I thought. Had Wilson, in his panic, simply made mistakes? Or had von Bek sabotaged the monster after he had visited us? I would never know.

There is a line in that great Skimling epic of the Second Ether—"We have searched every inch of charted Space and Time and found only ghosts and shadows." As I looked about me then I, too, saw only ghosts and shadows. Were we all simply reflections of some forgotten original, versions in an infinite series of men and women? How many million Bastables at that moment knew a scene almost identical to this? Was there any such thing as real individuality?

I was sure there was. I looked to where Mrs. Persson was comforting Dempsey. I was sure that Una Persson was unique. Able to move between the space-time planes of the multiverse, she had no counterparts and few equals. I wondered, with a kind of twisted hope, if the act of joining the League of Temporal Adventurers meant that all those ghosts and shadows of oneself were reincorporated or abolished. Was that the benefit Mrs. Persson had hinted at? And yet to know such a benefit was also to know a peculiar kind of loneliness.

Cossacks had now come up to help Professor Marek get the mechanical man on its feet. Its whole body was smeared with its creator's flesh and blood and the head was slightly dented, giving it a mad, crooked grin, but once it was on its feet it marched with easy precision between the Cossacks. Clearly, the thing had been tampered with—and Wilson's death was intentional.

The sense of being a courtier in some Byzantine power struggle was very strong. I have always hated such stuff at the best of times. I had the choice, once, of standing as the Liberal for Croydon, but I could not bear the thought of wasting my time extracting promises from people who had no clear intention of keeping them. But at least the corridors of Whitehall did not as a rule smell of freshly spilled blood!

Djugashvili was thoroughly satisfied with the day. His own brief expression of terror forgotten, he strutted up to Dempsey and put his arm around the airshipman. "Well, my friend, you have joined us. The bombs are aboard, eh?"

Dempsey straightened up, pulling away from the warlord's embrace. "They're aboard," he said. His voice had a colder, more controlled note.

Djugashvili was still in good spirits. His manner was jocular. "Then get to your ship, sir. Get up into the air, Captain Dempsey. Speed like the wind to your target. Your mission is a glorious one. You will redeem us. I wish to witness no further disloyalty to our great, common cause!"

Dempsey was shaking his head with open amusement at Djugashvili's hypocritical rhetoric.

"Ah!" The Steel Tsar lifted his head and seemed to taste the air and find it sweet. "What glory it holds for me, what fruits and rewards, what honour, this future I see!"

Mrs. Persson tapped him lightly upon the shoulder, causing him to turn, angered by the interruption. He followed her pointing finger, staring up into the sky.

"And here," she said, "is what you might call an alternative future, comrade."

The horizon was filling with airships, coming up over the wide line of the steppe until it seemed a vast thundercloud approached us. They had cut their engines and were using the prevailing wind. The old airshipman's trick had been perfectly timed.

The Cossacks were in temporary disarray, scrambling for their horses and vehicles, tearing the canvas from their artillery.

Then, in ragged unison, the engines of the Russian fleet burst into life and the ground shook to their roar.

It was the first wave—troop-ships bearing the aerial marksmen who preceded the arrival of the great flying ironclads.

Even as we stared, the gliding infantrymen began to pour

from the huge gondolas, sailing on wings of shimmering silk and firing as they descended.

I saw mounted Cossacks charging towards the flying infantry to be cut down by accurate fire from the carriers which hung low in the sky, offering light artillery cover. I saw horses and men fall in the light of the noon sun, sliced into red ribbons by the steady chatter of the aerial gatlings, their blood bright as their last night's dreams.

I turned my back upon the scene. Then we marched away, heading for the secret hangar. There, the *Vassarion Belinsky* stood ready in her lines, bearing the cargo from hell she must soon release upon the world.

I did not look at my companions. I did not want them to look at me.

In my heart of hearts I knew that I was planning to do all I could to change the course of history, to challenge the forces of fate and, if necessary, perish in the attempt.

CHAPTER EIGHT

Revolutions

To my surprise, Professor Marek hurried aboard with Djugashvili just as we were about to go aloft. The Steel Tsar's little eyes were bright with a kind of lust, but he went straight to the cabin he had made his people prepare for him. For a while at least, we were spared his company on the familiar control deck of the *Vassarion Belinsky*.

The hangar was lit by crude flares and not until Dempsey had given the orders to set the engines at idle did the Cossacks push back the great doors and let in the light. Then they took hold of the ropes and slowly eased the great ship out of the shed.

She began to tug at her confining ropes like a mastiff on a leash and at last we were in open ground.

Dempsey stood back with a courteous, half-mocking bow and allowed me to take the wheel. I did so naturally. "Let go the ground lines," I said.

My orders were relayed to the rough-and-ready crew below. I put the engines to half-speed and we began to rise into the sky, our turbines pounding like a single heartbeat, lifting effortlessly, light as swan's down, into the early afternoon. We had drawn most of our crew from a ramshackle bunch of half-trained Cossacks, some of whom were deserters from the Volunteer Airfleet. I murmured some uncertainty, but Dempsey reassured me. "They'll do for this work, old man, never fear."

Through the observation ports we were witness to the first clashes between Cossacks and Central Government troops. Taking cover where they could, the expert riflemen of the steppe were picking off the gliding infantry even as they left their vessels. They fell from the air like stricken moths.

Again I could do little but watch helplessly.

Dempsey took the wheel again. "There's nothing else but to let them get on with it," he said. "All right, height coxswain— put us up to five thousand feet: moderate ascent. Helmsman—" this to me—"North by north-west, if you please. Hold our speed steady as she goes."

She was a beautiful ship and did effortlessly everything we demanded of her. This dignified queen of the skies should never, I thought, have been employed in the foul work Djugashvili demanded of her.

"Let her take a point or two," Dempsey commanded. All at once he had become a capable airship captain—as he had been before he had helped commit history's worst single crime in the name of idealistic principle. Yet even if he bore no guilt, why, I wondered, had he agreed to bomb Makhno's camp? Was he making amends for something or was he determined to compound his crime? Had cynicism, that most cancerous of human qualities, consumed him completely?

Yet he was every inch the airshipman. His hands were hardly shaking at all as he stood on the bridge, now folding his arms across his chest, watching the ground fall away.

There was a strange air of calm aboard. We were still flying the Russian colours, so we were not attacked. It was, however, a very odd feeling to witness all that destruction taking place around us as we sailed through it, almost as if we, ourselves, were already ghosts…

Acting on Djugashvili's earlier orders, a wireless was sent out to the surrounding ships, giving our status and offering to join the battle. The warlord had anticipated the response. We were told to return to Odessa for fresh armaments and to report on our condition.

We sailed away from the main battle arena as the first flying ironclads began to heave their mighty hulls across the sky, while from their tubes burst deadly aerial torpedoes to wail earthwards and burst amongst the Cossack riders. Those reckless horsemen had no chance against the torpedoes. Horses and men went down in a blur of exploding scarlet and smashed bone. After a while, I refused to look out of the observation ports.

I felt obliged to ask the next question. "Dempsey," I said urgently, "do you honestly intend to drop those hell-bombs on another mass of innocent people? Are you really planning to kill Makhno and his followers?"

Dempsey turned his sad, self-mocking eyes on me. "Of course," he said. "I am the servant of Fate. I have no choice."

I still could not tell if he was serious.

"By what logic do you justify such an action, man?"

"By the logic of chance and random impulse, Captain Bastable."

"By the logic of savage nature!" It was Djugashvili coming up onto the bridge. He was flanked by two huge Cossack bodyguards.

Something had happened to his helmet. It seemed streaked with blood or rust, but he was oblivious of this further stigmatum, and for a moment I thought I was a different Bastable standing on the deck of a different airship and addressing a different Djugashvili. Images of those around me rippled outwards in a multitude of colours, many of them unrecognizable, and again I felt faint. I held tight to the wheel and pretended my full attention was on my steering. There was a mixture of sulphur and lemon in my nostrils, perhaps from some ointment the warlord used on his ruined face.

I could not rid myself of a terrible sense of inevitability, as if I must take part in this inhuman action over and over again, without hope of change. It was as if I had already descended into Hell. And did I already serve Lucifer? Such was the nature of my thoughts, for at certain times only the old descriptions serve. It could be that I was caught forever in this scene, doomed always to repeat actions which would lead to this moment, over and over again for eternity. This was the legendary fate of such mythical figures as the Flying Dutchman and the Wandering Jew. Was that why their stories retained their power? Because they told a fundamental truth of our condition?

At the same time I felt that many strange tensions were surfacing and, in manifesting themselves, might be explained or at least examined. I think that Time had become a little unstable, because of the attempted manipulations, and that we were all aware of an unusual and dangerous situation. We were infected by a demonic carelessness as if we actually were about to witness the end of the world.

I found it very difficult to concentrate on my undemanding task. I looked across at Dempsey and again experienced that scene, with O. T. Shaw, von Bek, Una Persson and the others, as the *Loch Etive* drove relentlessly through the skies, bound for Hiroshima.

Every so often I thought I noted von Bek on deck with us, but I never saw him directly. This was not the von Bek I had sailed with, so long, long, ago—and yet even now sailed with somewhere at this very moment—this was the albino "Monsieur Zenith", who had described himself as something of a sorcerer. I thought again of Teku Benga, of the supernatural forces which gathered there, and my rational mind refused to find answers.

Here, aboard the *Vassarion Belinsky*, commanded by a mad Georgian claiming to be a Cossack, I knew that neither our science nor our sorcery—nor, indeed, our swords—could affect one jot the power of the multiverse to continue reproducing itself, every action, every soul, every creature, infinitely. New Bastables were even now being formed from the raw stuff of Chaos. No action could stop this. Every action had its consequence, added to the proliferation of possibilities, added new dimensions to Time and Space.

"Are we anything other than curious maggots, burrowing through the rotting cheese of History," mused Professor Marek, fingering his face. Recent events had disturbed him deeply. "What do you think, Dempsey?" His look towards Dempsey begged him for any crumb of comfort. "Why are we doing this? Shouldn't we—"

"We survive," said Dempsey, paying attention to the distant Earth. We were passing over the great wheatlands, beginning to turn in a wide arc now that we were out of range of the Centralists.

I saw that the man had begun, silently, to weep. But he quickly took control of himself.

"You don't believe in cause and effect, then, captain?"

Dempsey shrugged off Djugashvili's question and the warlord did not pursue it. "What about you, Mrs. Persson?" he asked.

"Oh, I believe very much in cause and effect," she said, "but not in the linear sense. Every action has a proliferation of consequences. We can't remain alive without being responsible for thousands of actions and their consequences. We simply have to live with that fact and decide, morally if you like, how to formulate a civilized, secure environment for ourselves. So far we haven't succeeded."

Djugashvili was, obscurely, angered by this. He made a growling noise within his mask and stamped about the deck for a while. But she had less to hide from him now and pursued her point. "We think if we name something we control it."

"So we do. So we do," said the warlord, with disguised belligerence. "We make new names. Thus we control."

"It's an illusion. And a confusing one. It does nobody any good."

Even as she spoke I watched a hundred shadows break away from her and diffuse, like so many haloes, into the surrounding air. Yet still I felt that I was trapped. Still the airship roared on towards her obscene destiny.

"We make new names and thus create a new future," Djugashvili insisted. He glared out of the window and was disappointed in what he saw. "By this means we control both Time and Space! That is true power, Mrs. Persson."

"Neither is controllable." She shrugged. "One can only choose alternatives. Time and Space are constantly warping and recreating themselves. There is not the steady forward flow you so desperately need it to be, 'So-So', my dear—I tell you this merely for my own satisfaction. It can only seem to be that. The best we can hope for is to agree upon our joint hallucination!"

The Steel Tsar snorted and fidgeted. I thought he was regretting his decision to join us and witness Makhno's destruction. He kept waving his hand at Mrs. Persson, trying to dismiss what she said. "You intellectuals! You confuse everyone. It suits you. But you will not do the same to me! I give it the name. I control it."

"We can control only our own behaviour," said Mrs. Persson. Her voice was almost a whisper, yet brought silence with it. "Then we shall learn how best we can enjoy our existence in the multiverse. But if you try to control the multiverse, you risk that existence entirely. You will be doomed to repeat your efforts endlessly."

"The story of Tantalus!" Professor Marek giggled. His eyes darted from observation port to observation port. "Is each and every one of us carrying their own load, never reaching the end of their journey? Always frustrated. Always disappointed. Is this to be our human condition?"

"It is inevitable," said Dempsey. But Mrs. Persson clearly did not agree with him.

Suddenly I was struck at the strangeness of the conversation, as if we had all quite casually accepted our situation and now were merely curious to see how it would develop. Perhaps such knowledge gives one cause to lean a little towards the abstract.

"We can change," I said. "We can change something, surely?"

"Oh, certainly," said Dempsey sardonically, "if we wish hard enough, eh? The bulk of society, my dear old chap, is made up of people so cautious they believe it is a major upheaval if they have to change their address, let alone the fundamental basis of their beliefs! This caution is why it is so easy for our master, Djugashvili, and his kind to control us. They even get us to build our own prisons and create our own terrors. Caution is not a virtue in these times, Captain Bastable. It is very much a vice."

Djugashvili was fuming at the contempt in Dempsey's voice. "Be careful, sir! Be careful, comrade! There are more pawns than kings, sir, in this and every game we play!"

"Bah!" Dempsey offered the warlord his back. There was a strange, bleak anger in him now. Djugashvili had no notion of what was actually being discussed, but the words themselves had disturbed him quite badly.

Again it seemed to me that the scene changed and I occupied the command deck of the *Shan-tien,* heard Mrs. Persson's voice…

Parts of the city might be harmed…

Nonsense, I heard myself saying, *the city's nearly two miles away, Mrs. Persson.*

"City? What damned city?" Djugashvili was glancing from face to face, his cruel mask alive with his inner fury, his confusion. "What are you doing with this ship?"

"Sailing her as commanded," I told him almost casually.

"Take her down to a thousand feet, height cox. Easy as she goes."

"Makhno's camp isn't a city," insisted Djugashvili. His Cossack bodyguards both had their eyes tight shut. Clearly they had experienced these strange shifts and echoes also and thought themselves mad or dreaming.

Then von Bek had stepped into the centre of the control deck and was manipulating invisible lines. His bone-white skin was emphasized by the dark shadows which shivered around him with his every movement.

"Who in the Devil's name are you?" Djugashvili demanded, all uncertain bluster.

Von Bek smiled, made a further adjustment, and stepped from the scene. Mrs. Persson seemed puzzled. She reached out a hand and suddenly a thousand mirror images poured away from her, a thousand echoes, each as substantial as the last. I thought then that I came close to understanding something. Did each of us possess an archetype? And if so, how should we ever be reunited, each to their godhead, their Original Being, to stand again about the throne of our creator? Was there a way back for each one of us? Did this explain the hint of completeness which only just evaded me, as if one small element were lacking? Was I simultaneously, in dimension after dimension, performing this same action over and over again until I was able to make a change important enough to alter the pattern?

The *Vassarion Belinsky* continued her steady course. Djugashvili peered from the portholes, eager for a sight of the anarchist camp. He had refused to respond to what, I am sure, he regarded as his own hallucination. He rubbed at his eyes. He scratched at his exposed flesh. He moved his steel mask uncomfortably on his head and again the control deck was flooded with the stink of sulphur and lemons.

I found myself helplessly addressing the warlord. "What of your men, back there? Haven't you abandoned them?"

"What?" He had no interest in my question. It was as if he were puzzled by it, trying to recollect the subject. "Who?"

"Your men," I said. "They are leaderless. Shouldn't we return and help them. The Volunteer Fleet will wipe them out!"

"Yes, yes. But I want to see Makhno's end, not theirs!" He spoke in a reasonable whisper though his eyes were never quiet. "Where is the best view? And we should get some air. There are fumes in here. Smoke. It creates an optical distortion. You've noticed, of course."

"You intend to let your followers die?"

"I am with them in spirit. Wilson's mechanical giant leads them. It is down there now, giving them strength, giving them hope."

"It's a useless ikon."

"It's all they need. They need nothing more, Captain Bastable. Those chaps, anyway, have pretty much served their turn. They are an anachronism. You are a man of science, a modern man. You understand that those people are no longer of this age. History has no further use for them. Their attitudes hamper the advance of Scientific Socialism."

I could feel the blood draining from my face. "You are sacrificing those men, Djugashvili! They trusted you absolutely. You gave them the rhetoric and the goals to make them fight. They will not surrender—"

"I would not expect them to—"

"They could all be killed! For what?"

Mrs. Persson interrupted. She wiped sweat from her forehead and unbuttoned her greatcoat. The heat on the control deck seemed to be increasing. I even checked the engines, fearing one might be on fire, but could see no cause for the heat. "We're in a pretty unstable situation here, Captain Bastable. Watch your language, please!"

"But why must they die!" I knew I was being naïve, but I could no longer bear this savagery, this cold-blooded sacrifice.

"For History!" he said. "As I explained. The future is yours and mine, captain. Not theirs. They will die to ensure our future!"

Mrs. Persson's attention was on Dempsey, who had remained at his position for some minutes, staring steadily through the main observation port. She did not look at me as she spoke. "Here the idea of God has been replaced by the idea of the Future. The two notions are, admittedly, all but identical in the way in which they are self-contradictory and thus always fundamentally confusing to their worshippers, who must look to priests for translation, and so inevitably the priests (or whatever they call them) gradually take power…"

She was speaking rapidly in English. Djugashvili strode up to her and grabbed her arm. "What is this intellectual claptrap? We haven't time for any of that. It becomes increasingly important that we demonstrate our power to the Central Government. All this foolish talk is meaningless. Soon we shall rule the world. I will reward you, never fear. You'll be our first admiral, Captain Dempsey, a socialist hero. When the disaffected millions of the great cities rise to join us, we shall all be heroes. This demonstration will be in their name!"

Dempsey ignored him, coming back to check our instruments and murmuring to me. "Three-quarter speed, I think."

I relayed the order and felt the ship surge against the wind.

"You will lead our airships to Petersburg. You are a fine, brave man, Captain Dempsey. You, too, Captain Bastable. You will know every honour our nation can bestow…"

Not one of us listened to any of this. It was his usual way of attempting to manipulate us. He did not understand that we had all volunteered for this flight and that we each had our own particular motives. We all knew that every word of praise could as easily turn to hatred and that as soon as we had served our turn we, too, would doubtless be "liquidated" in the name of the future.

"Thank you, sir," said Dempsey. He looked towards Professor

Marek, who sat jotting down calculations on a pad of paper. "Anything unusual, professor?"

"I don't think so."

We were sailing through a great sea of greyness. Grey clouds surrounded us. A little rain was spotting the observation ports and we heard it drumming on our hull. Grey light filled the bridge, increasing Dempsey's pallor and emphasizing the unhealthy, peeling skin of Professor Marek. The ship at that moment seemed like a ship of the dead. It was as if we were already in Purgatory.

Dempsey, freshly alert, cocked his ear. "Do you hear a bit of a change in the note of the starboard engine, Mr. Bastable?"

I had heard nothing untoward, but I respected his judgment. Like any good airship captain, he was listening all the time. An airship's running depends as much on the ears as the eyes. It's the first thing they teach you. And so when Captain Dempsey told me to let him take the wheel, I obeyed at once. "Something wrong, Mr. Bastable. Could you go and check the nacelle?"

"Very good, Captain Dempsey."

As I went rapidly out of the flight deck into the main companionway I found to my surprise that I had been followed by Mrs. Persson. I opened my mouth to speak but she silenced me, motioning me to continue my way amidships but to stop at the central elevator leading to the maintenance warrens amongst our helium sections. Even as we traveled upward together in the elevator, she said nothing. I drew back the double door and stepped into semi-darkness. From somewhere above me came the familiar whistling of the upper currents, the odd, organic drumming and rushing, as if we listened to the innards of some mythological flying monster. All around us the inspection tubes, silver and brass and pewter, curled like intestines, while the rays which fell between the helium sections from two great translucent skylights overhead were liver-coloured and ominous. The sections would sometimes breathe, gasping in or out as if at whim to bar our path or to facilitate it as we negotiated the semi-rigid companionways between helium sections and reached the crowns. We stood with the wide cloud all around us now, separated from the abyss by a waist-high hand-rail of oak and brass, sailing at an altitude no previous generation had ever dreamed of achieving.

The engines were invisible below us. We felt their masculine vibrations as the mighty turbines pushed the *Vassarion Belinsky* on her stately progress through the upper air. Her gaudy flags snapping in her taut, glittering yards, she was as proud a craft as ever flew— but on her way to keep a *rendez-vous* with eternal dishonour.

Una's hair was blowing around her face like pale fire and her wonderful eyes looked steadily into mine. She smiled a little.

My mind was clouded again. I tried to grasp at small, immediate things. "How much further to Makhno's camp?" I asked her.

In all directions, we saw the cloud oceans, rising and falling in slow harmony. I wanted only to look upon this wonder in silence, with her in my arms. Now there was a mutual feeling. I knew it. I reached towards her.

"About half-an-hour." Her voice was impatient, urgent. "Captain Bastable—we have to disarm those bombs. We have half-an-hour—probably less—to do it. That is why we came up here. It is the one place they are reluctant to patrol—they have no air-sense, Djugashvili's men—and there's an emergency stairwell they don't know about. It starts up here and goes straight down. It's not guarded. It leads directly into the lower hold, which is now the bomb-bay."

I was dumbstruck. My own concerns—my love for her—my need to have some explanation for the 'ghosting' phenomena on the flight deck—gave way to a larger hope. A hope for all of us. Had I been offered a chance to change events, to stop the proliferation of this terrible crime? Had Mrs. Persson and her fellow chrononauts devised a means of turning the progress of the world back onto some saner course? But by what alchemy did they manipulate the very tides of the multiverse? What power was theirs, save the power of their own wills?

I needed to know one more thing. "Is Dempsey play-acting?" I asked her.

A great wave of white cloud washed over the rail and swathed her to her shoulders so that for a moment only her wonderful face was visible. "I don't know," she said frankly. "But I must say, Mr. Bastable, I feel very uneasy about his behaviour. It's as if he's phasing in and out of several personalities, several options, at the same time. That's never happened to any League member before. There are only old stories about it, in the early discoveries, when we were simply drifting into the unknown, hoping for currents and signs. So many died, fatally fractured. And Dempsey has the symptoms, I think…"

It was almost as if she had lapsed into a foreign language. I knew only the jargon of the soldier and the airshipman. The queer lingo, part science, part metaphysics, part meteorology, of the chronic philosopher-adventurers whose ranks I had been invited to join was mysterious—but learn it I must. In time I would discover that the chrononaut relies greatly upon the power of language to make some kind of ponderous progress through the unknown fractures and endless eddies of the multiverse and must learn more than twenty song-cycles in order to travel into a wide number of realms. Some vast zones will only open to a certain air, whistled lightly and purely upon the lips…

I said to her: "Madam, I believe your cause to be a just one. Your knowledge and experience in these matters being greater than mine, I ask you to put me at your service."

She took my hand and held it. "Thank you, dear friend," she said. I knew then that, no matter what else befell us, we should always be firm comrades. Then she was flitting like a ghost along the central walkway, her feet tapping on the crown like the ticking of a watch. "Quickly, Captain Bastable. This way."

She stopped, leaned down and lifted up a hatch cover. It fell back with a muffled thud. "Here it is. Down we go. I'll lead the way."

By the time I reached the hatch and put my feet on the ladder she was almost out of sight in the murk below. It seemed that we descended forever between the creaking gas sections until we were evidently passing down into the main decks. Then at last we found ourselves in the chilly interior of the lower hold. I heard the familiar creaking of the bomb-racks and I shuddered as, through the semi-darkness, I made out their long torpedo-like shapes. Mrs. Persson played an electric torch over them. The cases were crudely made, roughly standard in size and covered in Old Slavic phrases, decorated with the same peasant designs I had seen on Cossack finery, especially their weapons. They had a quaint, old-fashioned look to them, those bombs which threatened the destruction of the entire world.

Mrs. Persson moved towards them. The creaking bays opened and closed an inch or two, letting in light, then shutting it out again. "The detonating devices are in the noses," she said. "We have to unscrew them." Whereupon, without any further preliminaries, she slid herself out, straddling one of the bombs. A large wrench in her right hand, she immediately began to work on the device's nose-section. "You'll have to help me," she said. "Take this while I use the pliers."

Looking down as the flaps rose and fell, I began to doubt if the racks could accept our weight. I feared the whole of the lower hold would give way and carry us and the bombs with it.

We had been working less than five minutes before we heard voices from the gallery above us. I half expected a shot to ring out and to see Djugashvili and his men with smoking pistols in their hands, but it was Dempsey. He must have suspected us, otherwise he would never have left the bridge.

"There's no need for that!" He spoke out of the semi-darkness of the hold, his voice like the Wrath of God. "No need at all. Leave my bombs alone!"

"You've lost control, Captain Dempsey." Mrs. Persson continued to work on the nose-cone. "Have you really gone crazy? This was what we agreed we should do—"

"It was your plan, Mrs. Persson, not mine."

"It was the League's. Surely you aren't going to help Djugashvili kill those thousands of people? You have no clear idea of the power of these things. They could start a chain-reaction across the planet. As it is, you already know the kind of dimensional chain-reaction your original decision created…"

Dempsey drew his service revolver from its holster. "Move away," he commanded. "Stop what you're doing at once."

I had never seen Mrs. Persson so evidently frightened. "Captain Dempsey! You must not do this! Get a grip on yourself! You can't be responsible for this. Makhno—"

Defiantly, I threw my weight upon the wrench, feeling the nose-cone begin to shift. "Stop that, Bastable, or I shoot Mrs. Persson!"

This confronted me with a new dilemma. I paused, glancing from Dempsey to Mrs. Persson.

"Those bombs have to be detonated," Dempsey said. "Nothing else will do."

"But we intended to show that they didn't work." Una Persson was close to tears. "We have to stick to the original plan, Dempsey. It's all we can do now! Once we have proved the impotence of the bombs…"

"It will prove nothing!"

The gallery behind him was now crowded with armed Cossacks and it was clear we would have no chance in a fight. For a moment or two Mrs. Persson kept at her work and then, with a helpless sigh, she put down the pliers. "We'll have precious few chances again," she said. But she seemed to have reconciled herself to this turn of fate. She clambered back up and stood there as Dempsey's Cossacks swarmed around us.

A score of revolvers were leveled at us now. Slowly, Dempsey began to climb down from the gallery until he stood before us, holstering his own pistol. There was a silence in the hold. It was broken only by the creaking of the hatches, the melancholy howling of the wind outside.

"You can't be allowed to interfere with my future," said Dempsey. "And it is mine, Mrs. Persson. No one else's. I have the moral right to decide what to do with these—" He waved vaguely towards the garishly painted bombs. "Your plan, Mrs. Persson, saved the maximum lives. Mine will save the maximum souls."

"You'll make a nonsense of everything…" But she faltered, as if suddenly she understood what he intended to do. She frowned and drew up the collar of her military coat.

"I told you before, captain," she said. "You assume too much guilt. You have no right to this."

"More right than you, Mrs. Persson. And even a little more than Bastable!" He grinned at us—or rather he attempted to show us a grin. Perhaps by twisting his lips in that peculiar rictus, he meant to prove that he was mentally balanced. His wild eyes strayed back to the bombs. "All the right in the multiverse," he said. His manner and air were that of a fifteenth-century monk who had elected to league himself with the Devil. He was defiant. He was miserable. He was terrified. Whatever profound metaphysical battles were being fought across the multiverse, they were all of them mirrored in poor Dempsey's tortured psyche. His eyes begged us for death, for an end to his torments.

"Please, Captain Dempsey—" I murmured. I tried to appeal to the reason I knew was still in him but which his madness had at least momentarily conquered. "You go against all your training. You should be on the bridge. The ship has no master!"

"Oh, no," he said. "She has a master. Von Bek is at the helm. There's no finer pilot."

"Von Bek is a shade," I said.

"Oh, to you, perhaps." Dempsey turned his head so that he could not meet my eye. Like an old pike he had my measure and was refusing to take my bait.

"Djugashvili hasn't the experience or the nerve for the job!" said Mrs. Persson. "You've left this ship and its cargo in command of a brute."

"Von Bek is in command." Dempsey spoke rapidly to the Cossacks, some of whom ran to the storage lockers in the upper galleries.

For my own part, I knew a strange sense of peace. My mind was no longer confused and there was no action I could take. Yet, should an opportunity present itself, I would still attempt to complete our original plan—if only to save Makhno.

"What does Djugashvili think of this?" asked Mrs. Persson.

Dempsey's grin broadened. Now he seemed genuinely amused. "Unfortunately there was a loose cable in his cabin. It fell onto his bunk. Struck that helmet thing of his. Not so much an electric chair as an electric bed, I'm afraid. He would have appreciated the joke."

"So he died in bed, after all." Una Persson shrugged. "He always boasted that he would."

"Oh, he's not dead," said Dempsey. "Just a little forgetful. There's something I want him to see."

I was not used to such casual humour on the subject of murder. Sometimes I thought my fellow nomads were from a different age—the court of the Borgias, or some near-future where murder was once more a familiar resort as the fragile institutions of law and democracy were allowed to crumble. I know they saw me as rather pious and squeamish but I have discovered that one thing does not change in the perpetual proliferation of Time and Space and that is one's fundamental character. I could not imitate them.

Seeing my expression, Dempsey became quite suddenly calm. Almost apologetically he stretched out his hand to me. "It's all right, old chap. Really. The Dempseys were always on the side of the angels. Honest Injun!"

The Cossacks returned with two packs which were handed to us.

"That's your gliding apparatus," Dempsey told us. "Here, I'll show you how to put it on." He rubbed at his sunken eyes. His voice became suddenly weary. "I'm chucking you off the ship. It's either that or shoot you."

Mrs. Persson showed no reluctance now. She donned the apparatus almost cheerfully. "I still don't hold with this, Captain Dempsey. And my own responsibility here is morally dubious. But since you offer me no alternative, I bow to your version of Fate."

Having committed myself to her cause, I could only do as she did and follow her as we were pushed towards an emergency hatch, already standing open.

Dempsey remained where he was, watching us. The last I saw of him was his ironic salute. "Goodbye, old man," he said, "and good luck. I hope you get the chance to start again—"

Then with a great smack, Mrs. Persson struck the air and her silken wings opened beneath me, just as I, too, was thrust from the hatch into the air and felt my gliding apparatus come to life, arresting my wild fall through the skies and allowing me to turn and spiral like a hawk, high above the wide, Ukrainian steppe. Away to the south I could just see the glinting gold of some Orthodox dome, but to the west was nothing but rich and rolling land, enough land to feed the world. I kept sight of Mrs. Persson, whose black coat and dark blue wings gave her the appearance of some monstrous human-headed dragonfly.

I looked back to see the great bulk of the *Vassarion Belinsky* vanishing into the grey sea of cloud overhead, her black-

and-yellow flags brave and brilliant on her yards, her turbines growling with confident authority. And somehow, then, I felt that Dempsey was doing the only thing he could do and I respected him for following his own dark star to the bitter, inevitable end. But I prayed for Makhno, just the same, as I gave myself up to the wonderful sensation of free flight. I realized I was fulfilling mankind's greatest dream—to fly like a bird, as naturally and as joyously as if the air were our familiar habitat. Yet, slowly but surely, we began to lose height and, eventually, were dropping towards the coarse turf to land at last upon a grassy hillock. Mrs. Persson had more experience with the equipment than I. My ankle turned slightly as I landed, but the injury was not serious. I could still walk reasonably well. I began to help Mrs. Persson out of her equipment. She was grumbling. "The least he could have done was drop us near a town. Although in these parts they'd probably burn us as witches before asking any questions." She shuddered. "I'm an awful snob about peasants, I'm afraid."

I mentioned dryly that I thought those of her political persuasion had some sort of egalitarian duty to resist such prejudice. "Egalitarianism isn't about prejudices," she said, "it's about equal shares of power. It's the only means we have of steering some sort of even course through a future which is forever, by the very nature of the multiverse, unguessable. We have only institutions and a crude, fragile kind of democracy standing between us and absolute Chaos. That is why we must value and protect those institutions. And be forever re-examining them."

She stopped herself. "I'm catching a touch of your earnestness, my dear friend."

And then she embraced me, almost in anticipation of what happened next.

The wide steppe was suddenly bathed in brilliant light, as if the sun had broken through the cloud, and we bowed our heads before the brilliance, even as it began to fade.

We were looking up, to where the *Vassarion Belinsky* had disappeared, and we knew exactly what Dempsey had done and why he had not wanted the bombs defused.

A moment later the ground began to shake under our feet, as if an earthquake moved the whole planet, and we were flung down by a gigantic blow. The very air first whispered and rattled like knives, then shouted, then bellowed in vast agony. Then a hot wind blew over the grasslands and the wheat of Ukraine. That wind, I was sure, was all that was left of Djugashvili, the Steel Tsar, and Professor Marek, whose invention had begun a terrible war. I was sure that Captain Cornelius Dempsey's spirit soared free at last, as the ash and scraps of the great aerial liner fell slowly across the landscape.

And then, like some unearthly echo, a sound rose upon the world—a voice without words, without beginning or end, and yet it seemed to contain all our wisdom. It was almost a cheer. Then, little by little, it began to fade. The light dimmed. The grey clouds swathed the wide steppe. In silence, we began to make our way towards the north.

That night we sheltered in a herdsman's dugout. We could still smell the stink of the ship. I asked her if there were not some danger of after-radiation with these bombs. She assured me that Dempsey had been clever enough—especially if von Bek really were helping him—to phase the bombs into a neutral zone. All we had experienced was a minor after-shock, which had blown bits of the airship back into our own zone. "We'd be dead if that thing had gone off here," she said.

I told her that I understood, I thought, why Dempsey had done what he did.

She moved closer to me, for my warmth, and again we embraced. "I understand, too. But we had agreed on a different plan. A plan which would have saved his life and Marek's. This is just another loss, as far as I'm concerned."

She refused to explain exactly what she meant. When she began to cry I made some clumsy attempt to comfort her.

Next morning she seemed to have recovered her spirits and was striding, almost gaily, over the rough turf, pointing out the village ahead. "Do you think it's safe to approach?"

I told her I could not anticipate the welcome we would get but that we had little choice. We must throw ourselves on the mercy of the local people.

The wind blew her hair away from her face. She had a familiar glow to her skin again.

"Do you still feel bitter about Dempsey?" I asked. I had tried to convince her that the man had done the only thing he understood. He had sacrificed himself. He had refused to kill Makhno.

"The bombs," she said, "their inventor, the despot prepared to use them and the despot's servants are all gone now. But while that syndrome continues to exist, so will that particular event continue. I'd hoped to break it. To make a different ripple."

"But it is broken," I said. "Dempsey's sacrifice did that."

"No," she said. "Dempsey's sacrifice redeemed only Dempsey. This takes rather more effort than mere sacrifice and a show of willing, Captain Bastable. Dempsey knew that. He belonged to the League. He did not betray himself, I'm sure. But he betrayed the rest of us. It was self-indulgent of him to want to be such a hero. It was childish."

I thought her judgment harsh. I said: "Perhaps all our efforts to break the circle are doomed?"

"Perhaps," she said, "but we have no choice. We must continue to try. All we possess, after all, is a little faith."

The sky had become a great, welling purple bruise, offering both rain and sunshine. As we neared the village, we heard the church bell tolling. Then out of the gates came a group of riders on shaggy ponies. For a second I feared that they were the Steel Tsar's men. Then I saw they flew the Black Flag. They were outriders for Makhno and soon recognized Mrs. Persson, greeting her with whoops and loud laughter, astonished at the coincidence.

We rode back to Makhno's camp with lighter hearts. More news arrived. The Central Government would allow the anarchists to set up their own settlements across the Ukraine and would guarantee their protection. It was more than they had hoped for.

When we got to the great camp, Makhno was already celebrating. "Our anarchist experiment will be an example to the world," he said. "Once people realize it is possible to live with genuine self-government, they will follow us. It is all we ask."

He sat at the head of a long table. Overhead were moored the hulls of the great black cruisers. The anarchist battle-fleet had at the last moment gone to the aid of the Cossacks and forced the Centralists to agree a truce. We learned that the mechanical Tsar had failed those it led quite as thoroughly as the original. It had begun to run berserk again and had been felled by one lucky shot from a Cossack *ataman* who had fired from horseback. This symbolic death had turned the mood of the Cossack Host. Makhno had become a peace-keeper, helping both parties discuss the terms for truce. Everyone emerged, he told us, with honour and he was now celebrated as a great diplomat, an honest negotiator. He was greatly proud of this reputation. He would, I thought, make something valuable of it.

The Steel Tsar was now no more than gaudy pig-iron, testament to more than one dream of power that had failed to become reality. For a second or two I mourned for Peewee Wilson, destroyed by his own belief that his sad ambitions and a few poorly developed skills could create a secure and orderly world.

I drank to the spirits of the heroic dead. Only Mrs. Persson refused to join in this particular ceremony. At length I myself became bored with such maudlin stuff and went to join her where she stood on the edge of the camp, one hand on a mooring line, looking out at the steppe.

"Did Dempsey really die for nothing?" I asked.

"What good is a martyr, Captain Bastable? A martyr shows us the power of faith. But what if that faith is misinformed? While people believe in heroes and the magic power of an individual to save them from the human condition, they will never be free. We must learn to love and celebrate human fallibility, human variety, human courage—"

"But Dempsey was courageous. He wanted to make amends."

"To whom? To those millions he helped murder? The same millions you helped murder? They are dead and gone, Captain Bastable. They are dead and gone."

Her fist was white upon the line. Her voice was full of a weary melancholy.

I heard a movement behind me and saw Nestor Makhno limping up, a bottle in his hand. "I was wondering why you'd wandered off. Are we getting too noisy for our intellectuals?"

I did not bother to deny his presumption. I was no more or less than an ordinary English soldier, albeit a somewhat confused one.

Makhno had heard what Dempsey's instructions had been and he was grateful to us—especially grateful to Dempsey.

"Dempsey wished only to make amends," I said. "He said it was his right to do what he did. And, Una, it *was* his right."

Nestor Makhno leaned his back against one of the taut ropes. He moved limply, like a corpse on a gibbet. He was very drunk. "We are all guilty," he said. "We are all innocent. Only when we accept responsibility for our own actions do we become free. And only when every one of us accepts their share of responsibility will the world become safe for us all. Lobkowitz tells us this. Dempsey had an old-fashioned sense of honour. He destroyed himself because of it. Sometimes, as you say, Mrs. Persson, we must re-examine our ideas—look carefully at what 'honour' means, for instance."

She offered him a wan smile. "You enjoy this kind of

conversation, eh? I think you're right, comrade."

"Dempsey saved all our lives," I said. "That, surely, is worth remembering."

"He saved many lives," Makhno agreed. He was more sober now. He put down his bottle and began to pace about, looking up at the swaying, faintly lit hulls overhead. "It is true. But Mrs. Persson's plan might have saved more. While we compete with one another in that way—while we compete against ourselves, even—and while we blame one another for our misfortunes, there will always be such conflicts as the one we've just seen resolved. They go on forever. Violence creates nothing but violence, no matter what we call it and what the excuse. And so it goes, down all the centuries. Our experiment will show that this is not necessary. We shall be a guiding light for the people of the next century." He began to hum some old Ukrainian melody.

Somehow I was cheered by Makhno's words. At last I felt relieved of that terrible burden, that almost unbearable failure of faith in myself. That awful sense of bewilderment had gone and I had confidence, now, that I was indeed ready to join the League of Temporal Adventurers, perhaps to take Dempsey's vacant place and in my own turn make amends for his noble failures.

Eventually, the anarchist stumbled away, genially waving to us almost by way of a blessing.

I reached out my arms to Una Persson and we fell together like children, so glad of the warmth of our love, which kept all the loneliness in the multiverse at bay. I felt the events which began in the temple of Teku Benga were at last resolved. I could begin a new existence, learning how to move at will through the wild currents and waves of an infinity of dimensions. I again had a worthwhile task ahead of me, though I had no notion of what that entailed.

I trusted Mrs. Persson. She would be my mentor and my guide through the complexities of the ever-shifting tides of Time, the constantly changing, infinitely self-reproducing dimensions of Space.

I looked forward to perpetual uncertainty, perpetual change, perpetual love. A nomad of the time streams, I would explore a multiverse as complex and as subtle and as creative as my own mind. And I had a companion to help me.

I looked forward to life in an eternal present.

END NOTE

That's the story, Moorcock, as far as it goes. I now know far more about the League than I did and we have various "safe" zones where we rest and recuperate from our adventures. Our work is never completed and never will be. Our self-interest and the interests of the human race are all that guide us and, suicidal as I was when your grandfather first found me, I am completely dedicated to our tasks. The evil that we do does indeed live after us—it reverberates and is amplified throughout the multiverse— but the good that we do also lives on and, somehow, we maintain a ramshackle sort of harmony.

I hope this manuscript reaches you. I have a feeling it is the last you'll ever receive from me. The time for reviewing my own career, my own past, is over. I have more interesting things on my mind.

So I'll say goodbye, Moorcock, and hope that you, too, will one day find tranquility in an "eternal present".

Good luck, old chap!

CPT. OSWALD BASTABLE

Airshipman,
Somewhere in the Lower Devonian

EDITOR'S AFTERWORD

And that, as best I can present it, is the final story of Oswald Bastable. As many readers will know "The Steel Tsar" Djugashvili sounds remarkably like "the Man of Steel", that well-known ex-priest, the Georgian who chose for himself the name of Josef "Stalin". But then it is not uncommon, in all the worlds of the multiverse, for the same kind of personalities to emerge in roughly similar roles. What is usually more interesting is when, through altered circumstances, they appear in very different roles. Although I expect further visits from Mrs. Persson, I gather that there will be no more special news of Bastable now that he has joined the famous League. I am glad, however, to learn that he has found himself at last, found some sort of direction, and is reconciled both to his "crime" and his loss of home.

MICHAEL MOORCOCK

Yorkshire

June 1980

FOREWORD

Born in London in 1939, Michael Moorcock is a prolific and award-winning writer with more than eighty works of fiction and non-fiction to his name. He is the creator of Elric of Melniboné, the Eternal Champion Jerry Cornelius and Colonel Pyat, amongst many other memorable characters. He is also the author of the *Hawksmoon* series of science fantasy novels and the original *Doctor Who* novel, *The Coming of the Terraphiles*. He currently divides his time between Austin, Texas and Paris.

www.multiverse.org

CAPTAIN NEMO

The Fantastic Adventures of a Dark Genius

KEVIN J. ANDERSON

When André Nemo's father dies suddenly, the young adventurer takes to the sea and is accompanied by his lifelong friend, Jules Verne. Verne is thwarted in his yearning for action, while Nemo continues to travel across continents...

THE MARTIAN WAR

KEVIN J. ANDERSON

What if the Martian invasion was not entirely the product of H.G. Wells's vivid imagination? What if Wells witnessed something that spurred him to write *The War of the Worlds* as a warning? From drafty London flats to the steamy Sahara, to the surface of the moon and beyond, *The Martian War* takes the reader on an exhilarating journey with Wells and his companions.